Helen H. Gardener

Pray you Sir, Whose Daughter?

Helen H. Gardener

Pray you Sir, Whose Daughter?

ISBN/EAN: 9783337275181

Printed in Europe, USA, Canada, Australia, Japan

Cover: Foto ©Andreas Hilbeck / pixelio.de

More available books at **www.hansebooks.com**

PRAY YOU, SIR, WHOSE DAUGHTER?

BY

HELEN H. GARDENER,

Author of "Is This Your Son, My Lord?" "Pushed by Unseen Hands,"
"A Thoughtless Yes," "Men, Women and Gods," etc., etc.

BOSTON, MASS.:

Arena Publishing Company,

COPLEY SQUARE,

1892.

Life's Gifts.

I saw a woman sleeping. In her sleep she dreampt Life stood before her, and held in each hand a gift—in the one Love, in the other Freedom. And she said to the woman, "Choose!"

And the woman waited long; and she said: "Freedom!" And Life said, "Thou hast well chosen. If thou hadst said, 'Love,' I would have given thee that thou didst ask for; and I would have gone from thee, and returned to thee no more. Now, the day will come when I shall return. In that day I shall bear both gifts in one hand." I heard the woman laugh in her sleep.

Olive Schreener's Dreams.

Dedicated

With the love and admiration of the Author,

To her Husband,

*Who is ever at once her first, most severe, and most sympathetic critic,
whose encouragement and interest in her work never flags; whose
abiding belief in human rights, without sex limitations, and in
equality of opportunity leaves scant room in his great soul
to harbor patience with sex domination in a land
which boasts of freedom for all, and embodies its
symbol of Liberty in the form of the only
legally disqualified and unrepresented
class to be found upon its shores.*

Preface.

In the following story the writer shows us what poverty and dependence are in their revolting outward aspects, as well as in their crippling effects on all the tender sentiments of the human soul. Whilst the many suffer for want of the decencies of life, the few have no knowledge of such conditions.

They require the poor to keep clean, where water by landlords is considered a luxury; to keep their garments whole where they have naught but rags to stitch together, twice and thrice worn threadbare. The improvidence of the poor as a valid excuse for ignorance, poverty, and vice, is as inadequate as is the providence of the rich, for their virtue, luxury, and power. The artificial conditions of society are based on false theories of government, religion, and morals, and not upon the decrees of a God.

In this little volume we have a picture, too, of what the world would call a happy family, in which a naturally strong, honest woman is shrivelled into a mere echo of her husband, and the popular sentiment of the class to which she belongs. The daughter having been educated in a college with young men, and tasted of the tree of knowledge, and, like the Gods, knowing good and evil, can no longer square her life by opinions she has outgrown; hence with her parents there is friction, struggle, open revolt, though conscientious and respectful withal.

Three girls belonging to different classes in society; each illustrates the false philosophy on which woman's character is based, and each in a different way, in the supreme moment of her life, shows the necessity of self-reliance and self-support.

As the wrongs of society can be more deeply impressed on a large class of readers in the form of fiction than by essays, sermons, or the facts of science, I hail with pleasure all such attempts by the young writers of our day. The slave has had his novelist and poet, the farmer his, the victims of ignorance and poverty theirs, but up to this time the refinements of cruelty suffered by intelligent, educated women, have never been painted in glowing colors, so that the living picture could be seen and understood. It is easy to rouse attention to the grosser forms of suffering and injustice, but the humiliations of spirit are not so easily described and appreciated.

A class of earnest reformers have, for the last fifty years, in the press, the pulpit, and on the platform, with essays, speeches, and constitutional arguments before legislative assemblies, demanded the complete emancipation of women from the political, religious, and social bondage she now endures; but as yet few see clearly the need of larger freedom, and the many maintain a stolid indifference to the demand.

I have long waited and watched for some woman to arise to do for her sex what Mrs. Stowe did for the black race in "Uncle Tom's Cabin," a book that did more to rouse the national conscience than all the glowing appeals and constitutional arguments that agitated our people during half a century. If, from an objective point of view, a writer could thus eloquently portray the sorrows of a subject race, how much more graphically should some woman describe the degradation of sex.

In Helen Gardener's stories, I see the promise, in the near future, of such a work of fiction, that shall paint the awful facts of woman's position in living colors that all must see and feel. The civil and canon law, state and church alike, make the mothers of the race a helpless, ostracised class, pariahs of a corrupt civilization. In view of woman's multiplied wrongs, my heart oft echoes the Russian poet who said: "God has forgotten where he hid the key to woman's emancipation." Those who know the sad facts of woman's life, so carefully veiled from society at large, will not consider the pictures in this story overdrawn.

The shallow and thoughtless may know nothing of their existence, while the helpless victims, not being able to trace the causes of their misery, are in no position to state their wrongs themselves.

Nevertheless all the author describes in this sad story, and worse still, is realized in every-day life, and the dark shadows dim the sunshine in every household.

The apathy of the public to the wrongs of woman is clearly seen at this hour, in propositions now under consideration in the Legislature of New York. Though two infamous bills have been laid before select committees, one to legalize prostitution, and one to lower the age of consent, the people have been alike ignorant and indifferent to these measures. When it was proposed to take a fragment of Central Park for a race course, a great public meeting of protest was called at once, and hundreds of men hastened to Albany to defeat the measure.

But the proposed invasion of the personal rights of woman, and the wholesale desecration of childhood has scarce created a ripple on the surface of society. The many do not know what laws their rulers are making, and the few do not care, so long as they do not feel the iron teeth of the law in their own flesh. Not one father in the House or Senate would willingly have his wife, sister, or daughter subject to these infamous bills proposed for the daughters of the people. Alas! for the degradation of sex, even in this republic. When one may barter away all that is precious to pure and innocent childhood at the age of ten years, you may as well talk of a girl's safety with wild beasts in the tangled forests of Africa, as in the present civilizations of England and America, the leading nations on the globe.

Some critics say that every one knows and condemns these facts in our social life, and that we do not need fiction to intensify the public disgust. Others say, Why call the attention of the young and the innocent to the existence of evils they should never know. The majority of people do not watch legislative proceedings.

To keep our sons and daughters innocent, we must

warn them of the dangers that beset their path on every side.

Ignorance under no circumstances ensures safety. Honor protected by knowledge, is safer than innocence protected by ignorance.

A few brave women are laboring to-day to secure for their less capable, less thoughtful, less imaginative sisters, a recognition of a true womanhood based on individual rights. There is just one remedy for the social complications based on sex, and that is equality for woman in every relation in life.

Men must learn to respect her as an equal factor in civilization, and she must learn to respect herself as mother of the race. Womanhood is the great primal fact of her existence; marriage and maternity, its incidents.

This story shows that the very traits of character which society (whose opinions are made and modified by men) considers most important and charming in woman to ensure her success in social life, are the very traits that ultimately lead to her failure.

Self-effacement, self-distrust, dependence and desire to please, compliance, deference to the judgment and will of another, are what make young women, in the opinion of these believers in sex domination, most agreeable; but these are the very traits that lead to her ruin.

The danger of such training is well illustrated in the sad end of Ettie Berton. When the trials and temptations of life come, then each one must decide for herself, and hold in her own hands the reins of action. Edu-

cated women of the passing generation chafe under the
old order of things, but, like Mrs. Foster in the present
volume, are not strong enough to swim up stream. But
girls like Gertrude, who in the college curriculum have
measured their powers and capacities with strong young
men and found themselves their equals, have outgrown
this superstition of divinely ordained sex domination.
The divine rights of kings, nobles, popes, and bishops
have long been questioned, and now that of sex is under
consideration and from the signs of the times, with all
other forms of class and caste, it is destined soon to pass
away.

ELIZABETH CADY STANTON.

Pray You, Sir,
Whose Daughter?

I.

To say that Mrs. Foster was cruel, that she lacked sympathy with the unfortunate, or that she was selfish, would be to state only the dark half of a truism that has a wider application than class or sex could give it; a truism whose boundary lines, indeed, are set by nothing short of the ignorance of human beings hedged in by prejudice and handicapped by lack of imagination. So when she sat, with dainty folded hands whose jeweled softness found fitting background on the crimson velvet of her trailing gown, and announced that she could endure everything associated with, and felt deep sympathy for, the poor if

it were not for the besetting sin of unclean-
liness that found its home almost invariably
where poverty dwelt, it would be unjust
to pronounce her hard-hearted or base.

"It is all nonsense to say that the poor
need be so dirty," she announced, as she
held her splendid feather fan in one hand
and caressed the dainty tips of the white
plumes with the tips of fingers only less
dainty and white.

"I have rarely ever seen a really poor
man, woman, or child who was at the same
time really clean looking in person, and
as to clothes—"

She broke off with an impatient and disgusted little shrug, as if to say—what was
quite true—that even the touch of properly
descriptive words held for her more soilure
than she cared to bear contact with.

John Martin laughed. Then he essayed
to banter his hostess, addressing his remarks meanwhile to her daughter.

"One could not imagine your mamma a
victim of poverty and hunger, much less
of dirt, Miss Gertrude," he began slowly;
"but even that sumptuous velvet gown of

hers would grow to look more or less—let us say—rusty, in time, I fear, if it were the only costume she possessed, and she were obliged to eat, cook, wash, iron, sew, and market in it."

The two ladies laughed merrily at the droll suggestion, and Miss Gertrude pursed up her lips and developed a decided squint in her eyes as she turned them upon the folds of her mother's robe. Then she took up Mr. Martin's description where the laugh had broken in upon it.

"Too true, too true," she drawled; "and if she dusted the furniture a week or so with that fan, I'm afraid it would lose more or less of its—gloss. Mamma quite prides herself upon the delicate peach-fuzz-bloom, so to speak, of those feathers. Just look at them!" The girl reached over and took the fan from her mother's lap. She spread the fine plumes to their fullest capacity, and held them under the rays of the brass lamp that stood near their guest. Then she made a flourish with it in the direction of the music stand, as if she were intent upon whisking the last speck of dust from the sheets of Tannhäuser that lay on its top. A little cry of alarm and protest escaped Mrs. Foster's lips and she stretched out her hand to rescue the beloved fan.

"Gertrude! how can you?" She settled back comfortably against the cushions of the low divan with her rescued treasure once more waving in gentle gracefulness before her.

"Oh, no," she protested. "Of course one could not work or live constantly in one or two gowns and look fresh, but one could look and be clean and — and whole. A patch is not pretty I admit, but it is a decided improvement upon a bare elbow."

"I don't agree with you at all," smiled her guest; "I don't believe I ever saw a patch in all my life that would be an improvement upon — upon —" He glanced at the lovely round white arms before him, and all three laughed. Mrs. Foster thought of how many Russian baths and massage treatments had tended to give the exquisite curve and tint to her arm.

"Then beside," smiled Mr. Martin, "a rent or hole may be an immediate accident, liable to happen to the best of us. A patch looks like premeditated poverty." Gertrude laughed brightly, but her mother did not appear to have heard. She reverted to the previous insinuation.

"Oh, well; that is not fair! You know what I mean. I'm talking of elbows that burst or wear out—not about those that never were intended to be in. Then, besides, it is not the elbow I object to; it is the hole one sees it through. *It* tells a tale of shiftlessness and personal untidiness that saps all sympathy for the poverty that compelled the long wearing of the garment."

"Why, my dear Mrs. Foster," said Martin, slowly, "I wonder if you have any idea of a grade of poverty that simply can't be either whole or clean. Did—?"

"I'll give up the whole, but I won't give in on the clean. I can easily see how a woman could be too tired, too ill, or too busy to mend a garment; I can fancy her not knowing how to sew, or not having thread, needles, and patches; but, surely, surely, Mr. Martin, no one living is too poor to keep clean. Water is free, and it doesn't take long to take a bath. Besides—"

Gertrude looked at her mother with a smile. Then she said with her sarcastic little drawl again :—

"Russian, or Turkish?"

"Well, but fun and nonsense aside, Gertrude," said her mother, "a plain hot bath at home would make a new creature out of half the wretches one sees or reads of, and—"

"Porcelain lined bath-tub, hot and cold water furnished at all hours. Bath-room adjoining each sleeping apartment," laughed Mr. Martin. "What a delightful idea you have of abject poverty, Mrs. Foster. I do wish Fred could have heard that last remark of yours. I went with his clerk one day to collect rents down in Mulberry Street. He had the collection of the rents for the Feedour estate on his hands—"

"What's that about the rents of the Feedour estate?" inquired the head of the house, extending his hand to their guest as he entered. Mrs. Foster put out her hand and her husband touched the tips of her fingers to his lips, while Gertrude slipped her arm through her father's and drew him to a seat beside her. Her eyes were dancing, and she showed a double row of the whitest of teeth.

"Oh, Mr. Martin was just explaining to mamma how your clerk collects rent for the porcelain bath-tubs in the Feedour property down in Mulberry Street. Mamma thinks that bath-rooms should be free—hot and cold water, and all convenient appointments."

Fred Foster looked at their guest for a moment, and then both men burst into a hearty laugh.

"I don't see anything to laugh at," protested Mrs. Foster. "Unless you are guying me for thinking Mr. Martin in earnest about the tubs being rented. I suppose, of course, the bath-rooms go with the apartments, and one rent covers the whole of it. In which case, I still insist that there is no reason why the poor can't be clean, and if they have only one suit of clothes, they can wash them out at night and have them dry next morning."

The men laughed again.

"Gertrude, has your mamma read her essay yet before the Ladies' Artistic and Ethical Club on the 'Self-Inflicted Sorrows of the Poor?'" asked Mr. Foster, pinching his daughter's chin, and allowing a chuckle of humorous derision to escape him as he glanced at their guest.

"No," said the girl, a trifle uneasily; "Lizzie Feedour read last time. Mamma's is next, and she has read her paper to me. It is just as good as it can be. Better than half the essays used to be at college, not excepting Mr. Holt's prize thesis on economics. I wish the poor people could hear it. She speaks very kindly of their faults even while criticising them. You—"

"Don't visit the tenement houses of the Feedour estate, dear, until after you read your paper to the club," laughed her husband, "or your essay won't take half so well. College theses and cold facts are not likely to be more than third cousins; eh, Martin? I'm sure the part on cleanliness would be easier for her to manage in discussion before she visited the Spillini family, for example."

"Which one is that, Fred?" asked Mr. Martin, a droll twinkle in his eye. "The family of eight, with Irish mother and Italian father, who live in one room and take boarders?"

There was a little explosive "oh" of protest from Gertrude, while her mother laughed delightedly.

"Mr. Martin, you are so perfectly absurd. Why didn't you say that the room was only ten by fifteen feet and had but one window!"

"Because I don't think it is quite so big as that, and there is no outside window at all," said he, quite gravely. "And their only bath-tub for the entire crowd is a small tin basin also used to wash dishes in."

"W-h-a-t!" exclaimed Mrs. Foster, as if she were beginning to suspect their guest's sanity, for she recognized that his mood had changed from one of banter.

The portiere was drawn aside, and other guests announced. As Mrs. Foster swept forward to meet them, Gertrude grasped her father's arm and looked into his eyes with something very like terror in her own.

"Papa," she said hastily, in an intense undertone; "Papa, is he in earnest? Do the Feedour girls collect rent from such awful poverty as that? Do eight human beings eat and sleep — live — in one room anywhere in a Christian country? Does—?"

Her father took both of her hands in his own for a moment and looked steadily into her face.

"Hundreds of them, darling," he said, gently. Don't stare at Miss Feedour that way. Go speak to her. She is looking toward us, and your mother has left her with Martin quite long enough. He is in an ugly humor to-night. Go — no, come," he said, slipping her hand in his arm and drawing her forward through the long rooms to where the group of guests were greeting each other with that easy familiarity which told of frequent intercourse and community of interests and social information.

II.

Two hours later Gertrude found herself near a low window seat upon which sat John Martin. She could not remember when he had not been her father's closest friend, and she had no idea why his moods had changed so of late. He was much less free and fatherly with her. She wondered now if he despised her because she knew so little of the real woes of a real world about her, while she, in common with those of her station, sighed so heavily over the needs of a more distant or less repulsive human swarm.

"Will you take me to see the Spillini family some day soon, Mr Martin," she asked, seating herself by his side. "Papa said that you were telling the truth — were not joking as I thought at first."

Her eyes were following the graceful movements of Lizzie Feedour, as that young lady turned the leaves of a handsome volume that lay on the table before her, and a gentleman with whom she was discussing its merits and defects.

"I don't believe the call would be a pleasure on either side," said Mr. Martin, brusquely, "unless we sent word the day before and had some of the family moved out and a chair taken in."

The girl turned her eyes slowly upon him, but she did not speak. The color began to climb into his face and dye the very roots of his hair. She wondered why. Her own face was rather paler than usual and her eyes were very serious.

"You don't want to take me," she said. I wonder why men always try to keep girls from knowing things—from learning of the world as it is—and then blame them for their ignorance! You naturally think I am a very silly, light girl, but—"

A great panic overtook John Martin's heart. He could hardly keep back the tears. He felt the blood rush to his face again, but he did not know just what he said.

"I do not—I do not! You are—I—I—should hate to be the one to introduce you to such a view of life. I was an old fool to talk as I did this evening. I—"

"Oh, that is it!" exclaimed Gertrude, relieved. "You found me ignorant, and content because I was ignorant, and you regret that you have struck a chord—a serious chord—where only make-believe or merry ones were ever struck between us before."

John Martin fidgeted.

"No, it is not that. I would like to strike the first serious chord for you—in your heart, Gertrude."

He had called her Gertrude for years. Indeed the Miss upon his lips was of very recent date, but there was a meaning in the name just now as he spoke it that gave the girl a distinct shock. She felt that he was covering retreat in one direction by a mendacious advance in another. She arose suddenly.

"Lizzie Feedour is looking her best to-night," she said. "She grows handsomer every day."

She had moved forward a step, but he caught the hand that hung by her side. She faced him with a look of mingled protest and surprise in her face; but when her eyes met his, she understood.

"Gertrude, darling!" was all he could say. This time the blood dyed her face and a mist blinded her for a moment. She remembered feeling glad that her back was turned to everyone but him, and that the window drapery hid his face from the others, for the intensity of appeal touched with the faintest shimmer of happiness and hope told so plain a story that she felt, rather than thought, how absurd it would look to anyone else. She did not realize why it seemed less absurd to her. She drew her hand away and the color died out of his face. Her own was burning. She had turned to leave the room when his disappointed face swam before her eyes again. She put out her hand quickly as if bidding him good-night and drew him toward the door. He moved beside her as in a dream.

"After you take me to see the Spillini family," she said, trying to appear natural

to any eyes that might be upon her, " we —
I—" They had reached the portiere. She
drew it aside and he stepped beyond.

"There is no companionship between two
people who look upon life so unequally.
Those who know all about the world that
contains the Spillini family and those who
know nothing of such a world are very far
apart in thought and in development. There
is no mental comradeship. I feel very far
from my father to-night for the first time —
mamma and I. I have looked at her all the
evening in wonder—and at him. I wonder
how they have contrived to live so far apart.
How could he help sharing his views and
knowledge of life with her, if he thinks her
and wishes her to be his real companion and
comrade. I could not live that way."

She seemed to have forgotten the newer,
nearer question, in contemplating the problem that had startled her earlier in the
evening. John Martin thought it was all
a bit of kind-hearted acting to cover his
retreat. He dropped her hand. A man-
servant was holding his coat. He thrust
his arms in and took his hat.

"Will you take me to see the Spillini family *to-morrow?*" asked a soft voice from the portiere. A great wave of joy rushed over John Martin. He did not know why.

"Yes," he said, in a tone that was so distinctly happy that the man-servant stared. The folds of the portiere fell together and John Martin passed out onto Fifth Avenue, in an ecstasy.

He is willing to share his knowledge of life with me — of life as he sees and knows it — she thought, as she lay awake that night. He does not wish to live on one plane and have me live on another. That looks like real love. Poor mamma! Poor papa! How far apart they are. To him life is a real thing. He knows its meaning and what it holds. She only knows a shell that is furbished up and polished to attract the eye of children. It is as if he were reading a book to her in a language he understood and she did not. The sound would be its entire message to her, while he gathered in and kept to himself all the meaning of the words — the force of the thoughts. How can they bear such isolation. How

can they? she thought with a new feeling
of passionate protest that mingled with her
dreams.

III.

"Sure an' I'd like to die meself if dyin' wasn't so costly," remarked Mrs. Spillini, as she gazed with tear-stained eyes at the little body that occupied the only chair in the dismal room. "Do the best we kin, buryin' the baby is goin' to cost more than we made all winter out o' all three boarders. Havin' the baby cost a dreadful lot altogether, an' now it's dyin's a dreadful pull agin."

Gertrude Foster opened her Russian leather purse and Mrs. Spillini's eyes brightened shrewdly. There was no need for the hesitancy and choice of words that gave the young girl so much care and pain. Familiarity with all the mean and gross of life from childhood until one is the mother of six living and four dead children, does not leave the finest edge of sentiment and pride upon the poverty-cursed victims of fate.

"If you would allow me to leave a mere trifle of money for you to use for the baby, I don't — it is only —" began Gertrude; but the ready hand had reached out for the money and a quick "Thanky mum; much obliged" had ended the transaction.

"I shall not tell mamma *that*," thought Gertrude, and she did not look at John Martin. It was her first glimpse into a grade of life to which all things, even birth and death, take on a strictly commercial aspect; where not only the edge of sentiment is dulled by dire necessity, but where the sentiment itself is buried utterly beneath the incrustations of an ignorance that is too dumb and abject to learn, and a poverty that is too insistant to recognize its own ignorance and degradation.

"Won't you set down?" inquired Mrs. Spillini, as with a sudden movement she slid the small corpse onto the floor under the edge of the table. "I'd a' ast you before, but —"

"O, dont!" exclaimed the girl; but before her natural impulse to stoop and gather up

the small bundle had found action possible,
John Martin had placed it on the table.

"Oh, Lord; don't!" exclaimed the woman,
in sudden dismay. "The boarders'd kick if
they was to see it *there*. Boarders is different from the family. We could ate affen
the table afther, but boarders — boarders'd
kick."

"Could — do you think of anything else
we could do for you?" inquired Gertrude,
faintly, as she held open the door and tried
to think she was not dizzy and sick from
the dreadful, polluted air, and the shock of
the revelation, with all that it implied, before her.

Four dirty faces, and as many ragged
bodies, were too close to her for comfort.
There was a vile stew cooking on the stove.
The air was heavy and foul with it. Gertrude distinctly felt the greasy moisture on
her kid gloves as they touched each other.

"No, I don't know's they's anything *more*
you can do," replied the passive, hopeless
wreck of what it was almost sacrilege to
call womanhood. "I don't know's they's
anything more you could *do* unless you

could let the boarders come in now. They
ain't got but a little over ten minutes to eat
in, an' dinner's ready," she replied, as
she lifted the pot of steaming stuff into
the middle of the table and laid two tin
plates, a large knife and a bunch of iron
forks and spoons beside it.

"Turn that chair to the wall," she added
sharply to one of the children, who hastened
to obey the command. "They'll *all* have to
stand up to it this time. I ain't a goin' to
shift that baby around no more till it's
buried, now that I *kin* bury it. Take this
side of the table, Pete. I don't feel like
eatin.' You kin have my place 'n the ole
man ain't here. Let go of that tin cup, you
triflin' young one. All the coffee they is,
is in that. Have a drink, Mike?" she asked,
passing the coveted cup to the second
boarder. Gertrude was half-way down the
dark hallway, and John Martin held her arm
firmly lest she step into some unseen trap
or broken place in the floor.

When they reached the street door she
turned to him with wide eyes.

"Great God," she moaned, "and people

go to church and pray and thank God—
and collect rent from such as they! Men
offer premiums to mothers and fathers for
large families of children—to be brought
up like that! In a world where that is
possible! Oh, I think it is wicked, wicked,
wicked, to allow it—any of it—all of it!
How can you?"

John Martin looked hopeless and helpless.

"I don't," he said, in pathetic self-defense,
feeling somehow that the blame was personal.

"Oh, I don't mean you!" she exclaimed,
almost impatiently. "I mean all who know
it—who have known and understood it all
along. How could men allow it? How
dared they? And to think of encouraging
such people to marry—to bring into a life
like that such swarms of helpless children.
Oh, the sin and shame and outrage of it!"

John Martin was dazed that she should
look upon it as she did. He was surprised
that she spoke so openly. He did not fully
comprehend the power and force of real
conviction and feeling overtaken in a sin-

cere and fearlessly frank nature by such a knowledge for the first time.

"I should not have brought you here," he said, feebly, as they entered the waiting carriage which her mother had insisted she should take if she would go "slumming," as she had expressed it.

She turned an indignant face upon him.

"Why?" she demanded.

He tried to say something about a shock to her nerves, and such sights and knowledge being not for women.

"I had begun to feel that he respected me —believed in me—wanted, in truth and not merely in name, to share life with me," she thought, "but he does not: it is all a sham. He wants someone who shall *not* share life with him—not even his mental life."

"You would come here with papa, would you not?" she asked, presently. "You would talk over, look at, think of the problems of life with him,"—her voice began to tremble.

"Certainly," he said, "but that is different. It—"

"Yes, it is different; quite different.

You love papa, and it would be a pain to
you to keep your mental books locked up
from him. You respect papa, and you
would not be able to live a life of pretense
with him. You—"

"Gertrude! Oh, darling! I love you.
I love you. You know that," he said grasping both her hands and covering them
with kisses. She snatched them away, and
covered her face with them to hide the tears
which were a surprise and shock to herself.

"I should not have taken her there," he
thought. "I'm a great fool."

He did not at all comprehend the girl's
point of view, and she resented his. He
could not imagine why, and her twenty
years of inexperience in handling such a
view of life as had suddenly grown up within her, made her unable to express quite
fully why she did resent his assumption that
she should not be allowed to use her heart
or brain beyond the limits set for their exer-
cise by conventional theory. She could not
express in words why she felt insulted and
outraged in her self-respect that he should
assume that life was and should be led by

her, upon a distinctly different and narrower
plane than his own. She knew that she
could not accept his explanation, that it was
his intense love that wished to shield her
from knowledge of all that was ugly—of all
the deeper and sadder meanings of human
experience; but she felt unequal to making
him understand by any words at her command how far from her idea of an exalted
love such an assumption was.

That he should sincerely believe that as a
matter of course much that was and should
be quite common in his own life should be
kept from, covered up, blurred into indis-
tinction to her, came to her with a shock
too sudden and heavy for words. She had
built an exalted ideal of absolute mental
companionship between those who loved.
She had always thought that one day she
should pass through the portals of some vast
building by the side of a husband to whom
all within was new as it would be to her.
She had fancied that neither spoke; that
both read the tablets of architecture — and
of human legend on every face — so nearly
alike that by a glance of the eye she could

say to him, "I know what you are thinking
of all this. It stirs such or such a memory.
It strikes the chord that holds these thoughts
or those." But she read as plainly now that
this man who thought he loved her, whom
she had grown to feel she might one day
love, had no such conception of a union of
lives. To him marriage would mean a physical possession of a toy more or less valuable,
more or less to be cherished or to be set under a glass case, whenever his real life, his
real thoughts, his deeper self were stirred.
These were to be kept for men — his men-
tally developed equals. She understood full
well that if she could have said this to him
he would have been shocked, would have resented such a contemptuous interpretation of
what he truly believed to be a wholly respectful love, offered upon wholly respectful terms.
But to her, it seemed the mere tossing down
of a filbert to a pretty kitten, that it might
amuse him for a few moments with its graceful antics. When he tired of the kitten, or
bethought him of the serious duties of life,
he could turn the key and count on finding
the amusing little creature to play with

again next day in case he cared to relax himself with a sight of its gambols. She resented such a view of the value of her life. She was humiliated and indignant. The perfectly apparent lack of comprehension on his part of any lapse of respect in attitude toward her, the entire unconsciousness of the insult to her whole nature, in his assumption of a divine right of individual growth and development to which she had no claim, stung her beyond all power of speech. The very fact that he had no comprehension of the affront himself, added to it its utterly hopeless feature. The love of a man offered on such terms is an insult, she said, over and over to herself; but aloud she said nothing.

She had heard, vaguely, through her tumult of feeling, his terms of endearment, his appeals to her tenderness and — alas! unfortunately for him — his apologies for having taken her to such a place. She became distinctly aware of these latter first and it steadied her. They had reached Washington Square.

" Yes, that revelation in Mulberry Street

was a horrible shock to me," she said, looking at him for the first time since they had
entered the carriage ; "but, do you know,
I think there are more shocking things than
even that done in the name of love every
day — things as heartless and offensively
uncomprehending of what is fine and true in
life as that wretched woman's conduct with
the lifeless form of her baby."

He recognized a hard ring in her voice,
but her eyes looked kind and gentle.

"How do you mean?" he asked, touching her hand as it lay on her empty purse
in her lap.

"I don't believe I could ever make you
understand what I mean, we are so hopelessly far apart," she said, a little sadly.
"That an explanation is necessary — *that* is
the hopeless part. That that poor woman
did not comprehend that her conduct and
callousness were shocking — *that* was the
hopeless part. To make you understand
what I mean would be like making her understand all the hundreds of awful things
that her conduct meant to us. If it is not

in one's nature to comprehend without
words, then words are useless."

His vehement protests stirred her sympathy again.

"You say that love brings people near together. Do you know I am beginning
to think that nothing could be a greater
calamity than that? Drawn together by a
love that rests on a physical basis for those
who refuse to allow it root in a common
sympathy and a community of thought it
must fail sooner or later. A humbled acceptance of the crumbs of her husband's
life, or a resentful endurance of it, may result from the accursed faithfulness or the
pitiful dependence of wives, but surely —
surely no greater calamity could befall her
and no worse fate lie in wait for him."

Her lover stared at her, pained and puz-
zled. When they reached her door he
grasped her hand.

"I thought you loved me last night, and
I went away in an ecstasy of hope. To-
day —"

"Perhaps I do love you," she said; "but
I do not respect you, because you do not

respect me." He made a quick sound of dissent, but she checked him. "You do not respect womanhood; you only patronize women — you only patronize me. I could not give you a right to do that for life. Good-bye. Don't come in this time. Wait. Let us both think."

"Let us both think," he repeated, as he started down the street. "Think! Think what? I had no idea that Gertrude would be so utterly unreasonable. It is a girl's whim. She'll get over it, but it is deucedly uncomfortable while it lasts."

"Mamma, said Gertrude, when she reached her mother's pretty room on the third floor. "Mamma, do you suppose if a girl really and truly loved a man that she would stop to think whether he had a high or a low estimate of womanhood?"

The girl's mother looked up startled. She was quite familiar with what she had always termed the "superhumanly aged remarks" of her daughter, but the new turn they had taken surprised her.

"I don't believe she would, Gertrude. Why? Are you imagining yourself in love with some man who is not chivalrous toward women?" Mrs. Foster smiled at the mere idea of her daughter caring much for any man. She thought she had observed her too closely to make a mistake in the matter.

Gertrude evaded the first question.

"I once heard a very brilliant man say—what I did not then understand—that chivalry was always the prelude to imposition. I believe I don't care very especially for chivalry. Fair play is better, don't you think so?" She did not pause for a reply, but began taking off her long gloves.

"Which would you like best from papa, flattery or square-toed, honest truth?"

Her mother laughed.

"Gertrude, you are perfectly ridiculous. The institution of marriage, as now established, wouldn't hang together ten minutes if your square-toed, honest truth, as you call it, were to be tried between husbands and wives. Most wives are frightened nearly to death for fear they will become acquainted with the truth some day. They don't want it. They were not—built for

it." Gertrude began to move about the
room impatiently. Her mother smiled at
her and went on: "Don't you look at it
that way? No? Well, you are young yet.
Wait until you've been married three
years —"

The girl turned upon her with an indignant face. Then suddenly she threw her
arms about her mother's neck.

"Poor mamma, poor mamma," she said.
"Didn't you find out for three years *after*?
How did you bear it? I should have com-
mitted suicide. I —"

"Oh, no you wouldn't!" said her mother,
with a bitter little inflection. "They all
talk that way. Girls all feel so, if they
know enough to feel at all — to think at all.
They rage and wear out their nerves — as
you are doing now, heaven knows why —
and the beloved husband calls a doctor and
buys sweets and travels with the precious
invalid, and never once suspects that he is
at the bottom of the whole trouble. It
never dawns upon him that what she is dying for is a real and loyal companionship,
such as she had fondly dreamed of, and not

at all for sea air. It doesn't enter his mind
that she feels humiliated because she knows
that a great part of his life is a sealed book
to her, and that he wishes to keep it so."

She paused, and her daughter stroked her
cheek. This was indeed a revelation to the
girl. She had been wholly deceived by her
mother's gay manner all these years. She
was taking herself sharply to task now.

"But by and by when she succeeds in
killing all her self-respect; when she makes
up her mind that the case is hopeless, and
that she must expect absolutely no frankness in life beyond the limits of conventional usage prescribed for purblind babies;
after she arrives at the point where she dis-
covers that her happiness is a pretty fiction
built on air foundation — well, daughter,
after that she — she strives to murder all
that is in her beyond and above the petty
simpleton she passes for — and she succeeds fairly well, doesn't she?"

There was a cynical smile on her lips, and
she made an elaborate bow to her daughter.

"Oh, mamma, I beg your pardon!" exclaimed the girl, almost frightened. "I

truly beg your pardon! It — you — I —"

Her mother looked steadily out of the window. Then she said, slowly, "How did you come to find all this out *before* you were married, child? Have I not done a mother's duty by you in keeping you in ignorance, so far as I could, of all the struggles and facts of life — of —"

The bitter tone was in her voice again. Gertrude was hurt by it, it was so full of self-reproach mingled with self-contempt. She slipped her arm about her mother's waist.

"Don't, mamma," she said. "Don't blame yourself like that. I'm sure you have always done the best possible — the —"

Her mother laughed, but the note was not pleasant.

"Yes, I always did the lady-like thing,— nothing. I floated with the tide. Take my advice, daughter,— float. If you don't, you'll only tire yourself trying to swim against a tide that is too strong for you and — and nothing will come of it. Nothing at all."

The girl began to protest with the self-confidence of youth, but her mother went on. She had taken the bit in her teeth to-day and meant to run the whole race.

"Do you suppose I did not know about the Spillini family? About the thousands of Spillini families? Do you suppose I did not know that the rent of ten such families —their whole earnings for a year—would be spent on—on a pretty inlaid prayer-book like this?" She tapped the jeweled cross and turned it over on her lap. The girl's eyes were wide and almost fear-filled as she studied her handsome care-free mother in her new mood.

"Did you really suppose I did not know that this gem on the top of the cross is dyed with the life-blood of some poor wretch, and that this one represents the price of the honor of a starving girl?" She shivered, and the girl drew back. "Did you fancy me as ignorant and as—happy—as I have talked? Don't you know that it is the sole duty of a well-bred woman to be ignorant —and happy? Otherwise she is morbid!" She pronounced the word affectedly, and then laughed a bitter little laugh.

"Don't, mamma," said the girl, again. "I quite understand now, quite—" She laid her head on her mother's bosom and was silent. Presently she felt a tear drop on her hair. She put her hand up to her mother's cheek and stroked it.

"The game went against you, didn't it, mamma?" she said softly. "And you were not to blame." She felt a little shiver run over her mother's frame and a sob crushed back bravely that hurt her like a knife. Presently two hands lifted the girl's face.

"You don't despise me, daughter? In my position the price of a woman's peace is the price of her own self-respect. I did not lose the game. I gave it up!"

Gertrude kissed her on eyes and lips.

"Poor mamma, poor mamma," she said softly, "I wonder if I shall do the same!"

For the first time since she entered the room, the daughter appeared to appeal for, rather than to offer, sympathy and strength. Her mother was quick to respond.

"If you never learn to love anyone very much, daughter, you may hope to keep your self-respect. If you do you will sell it all—

for his. And—and—"

"Lose both at last?" asked the girl, hoarsely. Katherine Foster closed her eyes for a
moment to shut out her daughter's face.

"Will you ever have had his?" she asked,
with her eyes still closed. "Do men ever
truly respect their dupes or their inferiors?
Do you truly respect anyone to whom you
are willing to deny truth, honor, dignity?
Is it respect, or only a tender, pitying love
we offer an intellectual cripple—one whose
mental life we know to be, and desire to
keep, distinctly below our own? Do—"
She opened her eyes and they rested on an
onyx clock. She laughed. "Come, daughter," she said, "it is time to dress for the
Historical Club's annual dinner. You know
I am one of the guests of honor to-day.
They honor me so truly that I am not per-
mitted to join the club or be ranked as a
useful member at all. My work they accept
—flatter me by praising in a lofty way; but
I can have no status with them as an histo-
rian—I am a woman!"

Gertrude sprang to her feet. Her eyes
flashed fire.

"Don't go! I wouldn't allow them to —"

The door opened softly. Mr. Foster's face appeared.

"Why, dearie, aren't you ready for the Historical Club? I wouldn't have you late for anything. You know I, as the vice-president, am to respond to the toast on, 'Woman: the highest creation, and God's dearest gift to mankind.' It wouldn't look well if you were not there."

"No, dear," she said, without glancing at Gertrude. "It would not look well. I'll be ready in a minute. Will you help me, Gertrude?"

"Yes," said the girl, and her deft fingers flew at the task. When the door closed behind her mother and the carriage rolled away, she threw herself face down on the bed and ground her teeth. "Shall I float, or try to swim up stream?" she said, to herself. "Will either one pay for what it will cost? Shall —"

"Miss Gertrude, dinner is served," said the maid; and she went to the table alone.

"To think that a visit to the Spillini family should have led to all this," she thought,

and felt that life, as it had been, was over
for her.

Aloud she said: —

"James, the berries, please, and then you
may go."

And James told Susan that in his opinion
the man that got Miss Gertrude was going
to get the sweetest, simplest, yieldingest
girl he ever saw except one, and Susan
vowed she could not guess who that one
was.

But apparently James did not wholly believe her, for he essayed to sportively poke
her under the chin with an index finger that
very evidently had seen better days prior to
having come into violent contact with a
base ball, which, having a mind and a curve
of its own, had incidentally imparted an ec-
centric crook to the unfortunate member.

"Don't you dast t' touch me with that old
pot hook, er I'll scream," exclaimed Susan,
dodging the caress. "I don't see no sense
in a feller gettin' hisself all broke up that a
way," and Susan, from the opposite side of
the butler's table, glanced admiringly at her
own shapely hand, albeit the wrist might

have impressed fastidious taste as of too
robust proportions, and the fingers have
suggested less of flexibility than is desirable.

But to James the hand was perfect, and
Susan, feeling her power, did not scruple to
use it with brutal directness. She had that
shivering dislike for deformity which is possessed by the physically perfect, and she
took it as a private grievance that James
should have taken the liberty to break one
of his fingers without her knowledge and
consent. Until he had met her, James had
carried his distorted member as a badge of
honor. No warrior had worn more proudly
his battle scars. For, to James, to be a
catcher in a base ball club was honor
enough for one man, and he had never
dreamed of a loftier ambition. He had
grown to keep that mutilated finger ever to
the fore as a retired general might carry an
empty sleeve. It gave distinction and told
of brave and lofty achievement, so James
thought.

Susan had modified his pride in the dis-
located digit, but he had not yet learned to

keep it always in the background. It had several times before interfered with his love-making, and James was humble.

"Oh, now, Susie, don't you be so hard on that there old base-ball finger! I didn't know it was a-going to touch your lovely dimple," and he held the offending member behind his back, as he slowly circled around the table towards the haughty Susan. "By gum! I b'lieve I left a mark on your chin. Lemme see." She thought she understood the ruse, but when he kissed her she pretended deep indignation and flounced out of the room, but the look on her face caused James to drop his left eyelid over a twinkling orb and shake his sides with satisfaction as he removed the dishes after Miss Gertrude had withdrawn from the dining room.

IV.

The visit to the Spillini family had, indeed, led to strange complications and far-reaching results. No one who had known young Selden Avery and his social life would ever have suspected him, or any member of his set, of a desire to take part in what, by their club friends or favorite reviews, was usually alluded to as the "dirty pool of politics." For the past decade political advancement, at least in New York, had grown to be looked upon by many as a mere matter of purchase and sale, and as quite beneath the dignity of the more refined and cultured men. It had been heralded as a vast joke, therefore, when young Selden Avery, the representative of one of the most cultured families and the honored son of an honored ancestry, had suddenly announced himself as a candidate for the Assembly. His club friends guyed

him unmercifully. "We never did believe
that you were half as good as you pretended
to be, Avery," said one of them, the first
time he appeared at the club after his nomination, "but I don't believe a man of us
ever suspected you of the depths of de-
pravity that this implies. What ever did
put such a ridiculous idea into such a level
and self-respecting head? Out with it!"

Banter of this nature met him on every
hand. He realized more fully than ever
how changed the point of view had grown
to be from the historical days of Washington or even of Lincoln. He recalled the
time when in his own boyhood his honored
father had served in the Legislature of his
native state, and had not felt it other than
a crowning distinction. Nor had it been so
looked upon then by his associates.

Nevertheless the constant jokes and gibes,
which held something of a real sting, had
become so frequent that young Avery felt
like resenting his friends' humorous thrusts.

"I can't see that I need be ashamed to
follow in the footsteps of my father," he
said, a little hotly. "Some of the noblest of

men—those upon whom the history of this
country depends for lustre—held seats in
the Assembly, and helped shape the laws of
their states. I don't see why I need apolo-
gize for a desire to do the same."

"It used to be an association of gentlemen up at the state capital, my boy. To-
day it is—Lord! you know what it is, I
guess. But if you don't, just peruse this
sacred volume," laughed his friend, sarcasti-
cally, producing a small pamphlet.

"Looks to me as if you'd be rather out
of your element with your colleagues.
'M-m-m! Yes, here is the list. Hunted
this up after I heard you were going to
stand for your district."

The English form of expression was no
affectation, for the speaker was far more
familiar with political nomenclature abroad
than at home. He would have felt it an
honor to a man to be called upon to "stand"
for his constituency in London, but to "run"
for it in New York was far less dignified.
Standing gave an idea of repose; running
was vulgar. Then, too, the State Legislature did not bear the proportionate rela-

tionship to Congress that the Commons did to Parliament, and it was always in connection with that latter body that he had associated the term.

"Let me see. One, two, three, four, 'teen 'steen—yes, I thought I was right! Just exactly nineteen of your nearest colleagues are saloon keepers. One used to keep that disorderly house on Prince Street, four are butchers, one was returned because he had won fame as a base-ballist and—but why go further? Here, Martin, I'm trying to convince Avery that it will be a trifle trying on his nerves to hobnob with the new set he's making for. Don't you think it is rather an anti-climax from the Union to the lower house at Albany? Ye gods!" and he laughed, half in scorn and half in real amusement.

John Martin had extended his hand for the small pamphlet of statistics. He ran his eye over the list, and then turned an amused face upon Avery.

"Think you'll like it?" he asked, dryly. Or are you taking it as my French friend here says his countrymen take heaven?"

"How's that?" queried Avery, smiling.
"In broken doses—or not at all?"

The French gentleman stood with that
poise which belongs to the successful man.
He glanced from one to the other and spread
his hands to either side.

"All Frenchmen desire to go to ze heaven,
zhentlemen. Why? Ah, zere air two at-
traczions which to effrey French zhentle-
man air irresisteble. Ze angels—zey air
women—and I suppose zat ze God weal
also be an attraczion. Ees eet not so?"

Every one in the group laughed and he
went gravely on.

"I zink zat eet ees true—ees eet not?—zat
loafly woman will always be vara much ob-
searved even in ze heaven eef we zhentlemen
are zere. Eef?" He cast up the corners
of his eyes, and made another elaborate
movement of his hands.

The others all laughed again.

"Yes, zhentlemen, ze true Frenchman
cares for two zings: a new sensation—
somesing zey haf not before experienced,
—and zat ees God; and for zat which zey

haf obscarved, but of which zey can naavear obscarve enough — loafly woman!"

The explosion of laughter that greeted this sally brought about them a number of other gentlemen, and the talk drifted into different channels Presently young Avery glanced at his watch and started, with rather a sore heart, toward the door. He remembered that he had promised the managers of his campaign that he would be seen that evening at a certain open-air garden frequented by the humbler portion of his constituency. He concluded to go alone the first time that he might the better observe without attracting too much attention. This plan was thought wise to enable him to meet the exigencies of the coming campaign when he should be called upon to speak to this element of his supporters.

Once outside the club house, he took a card from his pocket and glanced at the directions he had jotted upon it.

"I'll walk across to the elevated," he thought, "and make my connection for Grady's place that way. It will save time and look more democratic.

V.

The infinite pathos of life was never better illustrated, perhaps, than in the merry-making that night at Grady's Pavilion. The easy camaradarie between conscious and unconscious vice; the so-evident struggle the young girls had made to be beautiful and stylish, and the ghastly result of their cheap and incongruous finery; their ignorant acceptance of leers that meant to them honest admiration or affection, and to others meant far different things; their jolly, thoughtless, eager effort to get something joyful out of their narrow lives; the brilliant tints in which they saw the future, and the ghastly light in which it stood revealed to older and more experienced eyes, would have combined to depress a heart less tender and a vision less clear than could have been attributed to Selden Avery. Not that Grady's Pavilion was a bad place. Many of the girls present would not have been there had it been known as anything short of quite respectable; but it was a free and easy place, where vice meets ignorance without having first made an appointment, where opportunity shakes the ungloved hand of youth and leaves a stain upon the tender palm too deep and dark for future tears to wash away.

"I wonder if I am growing morbid," mused Avery, as he sighed for the third time while looking at the face of a girl not over eighteen years old, but already marked by lines that told of a vaguely dawning comprehension of what the future held for her. Her round-eyed companion, a girl with a childish mind and face, sat beside her, but all the world was bright to her. Life held a prince, a fortune and a career which would be hers one day. She had only to wait, look pretty, and be ready when the apple of fortune fell. Her part was to hold out a pretty apron to break its descent.

"Oh, the infinite pathos of youth!" muttered Avery, feeling himself very old with his thirty years of wider experience as his eyes turned from one girl to the other. "It is hard to tell which is the sadder sight; the disillusioned one or the one who will be even more roughly awakened to-morrow."

His heart ached whenever he studied the face of a young girl. "There is nothing so sad in all the wretched world," he sometimes said, "as the birth of a girl in this grade of life. I am not sure that the nations we look upon as barbarous because they strangle the little things before they are able to think — I am not at all sure that they are not more civilized than we after all. We only maim them with ignorance and utter dependence, and then turn them out into a life where either of these alone is an incalculable curse, and the combination is as fatal as fire in a field of ripened grain."

The younger girl was looking at him. Her wide expectant eyes rested on his face with a frankness and interest that touched his mood anew.

"Poor little·thing," he said, half aloud; "if I were to see her bound hand and foot and cast into a den of wolves, I might hope

to rescue her; but from this, for such as she
there is absolutely no escape.   How dare
people bring into the world those who must
suffer?"

"Huh?" said a voice beside him.   He had
spoken in a semi-audible tone, and his neighbor had responded after his habitual fashion,
to what he looked upon as an overture to
conversation.

"I did not intend to speak aloud," said
Avery, turning to glance at the man beside
him; "but I was just wondering how people
dared to have children — girls particularly."

The man beside him turned his full face
upon him and examined him critically from
head to foot.   Then he laughed.   It was
the first time he had ever heard it hinted
that it was not a wholly commendable thing
to bring as many children into the world as
nature would permit.   His first thought had
been that Avery was insane, but after looking at him he decided that he was only
a grim joker.

"I reckon they don't spend no great deal
of time prayin' over the subject," he said,
laughing again.   Then he crossed his legs

and added, "an I don't suppose they get
any telegrams tellin' them they're goin'
to *be* girls, neither. If they did, a good
many men would lick the boy that brought
the despatch, for God knows most of us
would a darn sight ruther have boys."

The laugh had died out of his voice, and
there was a ring of disappointment and
aggrieved trouble in it. Selden Avery
shifted his position.

"I was not looking at it from the point of
view of the parents of unwelcome girls," he
said, presently, "but from the outlook of the
girls of unwelcome parents. The reckon-
ing from that side looks to me a good deal
longer than the other." His voice was
pleasant, but his eyes looked perplexed and
determined. His neighbor began to readjust his opinion of Avery's sanity, and
moved his chair a little farther away before
he spoke.

"Got any childern of your own?" he
inquired, succinctly. Avery shook his head.
The man drew down the corners of his
mouth in a contemptuous grimace. "I
thought not. If you had, you'd take it a

darn sight easier. Childern are an ungrat-
ful lot. They're never satisfied—or next to
never. They think you're made for their
comfort instead of their bein' for yours.
I've got nine, and I know what I'm talkin'
about. If you've got any sympathy to
throw away don't waste it on childern.
Parents, in these days of degenerate young-
sters, are passin' around the hat for sympathy. In my day it was just the other way.
If one of the young ones went wrong,
people pitied the father and blamed the
child. Now-a-days they blame the father
and weep over the young one that makes
the mischief. It makes me mad."

He shut his teeth with a suddenness that
suggested a snap, and flashed a defiant look
about the room.

Avery glanced at his heavy, stubborn face,
and decided not to reply. He was in no
mood for controversy. And what good
could it do, he said to himself, to argue with
a mere lump of selfish egotism?

"That is an unusually pretty girl over by
the piano," he said, in a tone of mild indiffer-

ence which he hoped would serve as a period
to the conversation.

"She's Tom Berton's girl," was the quick
reply. "Berton's up to Albany most o' the
time, with me. I represent our district.
She's a nice little thing. She'll do anything
you ask her to. I never see her equal for
that. It's easier for her to do your way than
it is to do her own. She likes to; so everybody likes her. I wish I had one like her;
but my girls are as stubborn as mules.
They won't drive, and they won't lead, and
they'd ruther kick than eat. I don't know
where they got it. Their mother wasn't half
so bad that way, and the Lord knows it ain't
in *my* family. The girl she's with is one o'
mine. She looks like she could eat tenpenny
nails. She might be just as pretty an' just
as much liked as Ettie Berton, but she ain't.
She's always growlin' about somethin'. I'll
bet a dollar she'll growl about this when we
get home. Ettie will think it was splendid.
She'd have a good time at a funeral; but
that girl of mine 'll get me to spend a dollar
to come here and then she'll go home dissatisfied. It won't be up to what she expected.

Things never are. She's always lookin' to find things some other way. Now, what would you do with a girl like that?" he asked suddenly. Then without waiting for a reply, he added, "I give her a good tongue lashin', an' as she always knows it's comin', she's got so she don't kick *quite* so much as she used to, but she just sets an' looks sullen like that. It makes me so mad I could —"

He did not finish his remark, but got up and strolled away without the formality of an adieu.

Avery watched his possible future colleague until he was lost in the crowd, and then he walked deliberately over to where the two girls stood.

"I have been talking with your father," he said, smiling and bowing to the older girl, "and although he did not say that I might come and talk to you, he told me who you were, and I think he would not object."

"Oh, no; he wouldn't object," said the younger girl, eagerly. "Would he Fan? Everybody talks here. He told me so before we came. It's the first time we've been;

but he's been before. I think it's splendid, don't you?"

The older girl had not spoken. She was looking at Selden Avery with half suppressed interest and embryonic suspicion. She still knew too little of life to have formed even a clearly defined doubt as to him or his intentions in speaking to them. She was less happy than she had expected to be when she dressed to come, with her ever-dawning hope for a real pleasure. She thought there must be something wrong with her because things never seemed to come up to her expectations. She supposed this must be "society," and that when she got used to it, she would enjoy it more. But somehow she had wanted to resent it the first time a man spoke to her, and then, afterward, she was glad she did not, for he had danced with Ettie twice, and Ettie had said it was a lovely dance. She had made up her mind to accept the next offer she had, but when it came, the eyes of the man were so beady-black, and the odor of bay rum radiated so insistently from him that she declined. She hated bay rum because the worst

scolding her father ever gave her was
when she had emptied his cherished bottle
upon her own head. The odor always
brought back the heart-ache and resentment
of that day, and so she did not think she
cared to dance just then.

Selden Avery looked at Ettie. He did
not want to tell her what he did think and
he had not the heart to dampen her ardor,
so he simply smiled, and said: —

"It is my first visit here, too; and I don't
know a soul. I noticed you two young
ladies a while ago, and spoke of you to the
gentleman next to me and it chanced
to be your father"—he turned to the older
girl again— "so that was what gave me
courage to come over here. If I had
thought of it before he left me, I'd have
asked him to introduce me, but I'm rather
slow to think. My name is Selden Avery."

"Did father tell you mine?" she asked,
looking at him steadily, with eyes that held
floating ends of thoughts that were never
formed in full.

"No, he didn't," replied Avery, laughing
a little. "He told me yours, though," turn-

ing to the merry child at his side. "Ettie
Berton, Tom Berton's daughter."

Ettie laughed, and clapped her hands
together twice.

"Got it right the first time! But what
did he give me away for and not her? She
is Francis King. That is, her father's
name's King, but she is so awfully particular about things and so hard to suit she
ought to be named Queen, I tell her, so
I call her Queen Fan mostly." There was
a little laugh all around, and Avery said:—

"Very good, very good, indeed;" but
Francis looked uncomfortable and so he
changed the subject. Presently she looked
at him and asked:—

"Do you think things are ever like they
are in books? Do you think this is? She
waved her hand toward the music and the
lights. "In the books I have read—and
the story papers—it all seems nicer than
this and—and different. It is because I
say that, that they all make fun of me
and call me Queen Fan, and father says—"
she paused, and a cold light gathered in her
eyes. "He don't like it, so I don't say it

much, now. He says it's all put on; but
it ain't. Everything does seem to turn out
so different from what you expected—from
the way you read about. I've not felt like I
thought *maybe* I should to-night because—
because—" She stopped again.

"Because why?" asked Avery, laughing
a little. "Because I'm not a bit like the
usual story-book prince you ought to have
met and—?"

She smiled, and Ettie made a droll little
grimace.

"No, it wasn't that at all. I've been
thinking most all evening that it wasn't
worth—that—"

"Oh, she's worried," put in Ettie, "because she got her father to spend a dollar to
bring her. She's afraid he'll throw it up to
her afterward, and she thinks it won't pay
for that, so it spoils the whole thing before
he does it—just being afraid he will. But I
tell her he won't, this time. I—" Francis'
eyes had filled with tears of mortification,
and Avery pretended not to have heard. He
affected a deep interest in the music.

"Do you know what it is they are playing

now?" he asked, with his eyes fixed upon
the musicians. "I thought at first that it
was going to be — No, it is — 'Pon my word
I can't recall it, and I ought to know what it
is, too. The first time I ever heard it, I
remember —"

He turned toward where Francis had
stood, but she was gone. "Why, what has
become of Miss King?" he asked of the
other girl. Ettie looked all about, laughed
and wondered and chattered as gaily as a
bird.

"I expect she's gone home. She's the
queerest you ever saw. I guess she didn't
want me to say that about her pa. But it'll
make him madder than anything if she has
gone that way. He won't like it at all — an'
I can't blame him. What's the use to be so
different from other folks?" she inquired,
sagely, and then she added, laughing: "I
don't know as she is so different, either. We
all hate things, but we pretend we don't.
Don't you think it's better to pretend to like
things, whether you do or not?"

"No," replied Avery, beginning to look
with surprise upon this small philosopher

who had no conception of the worldly wisdom of her own philosophy.

"I do," she said, laughing again. "It goes down better. Everybody likes you better. I've found that out already, and so I pretend to like everything. Of course I do like some of 'em, and some I don't, but it's just as easy to *say* you like 'em all." She laughed again, and kept time with her toe on the floor.

"Just what don't you like?" asked Avery, smiling. "Won't you tell me, truly? I won't tell anyone, and I'd like to be sure of one thing you object to — on principle."

"Well, tob— Do you smoke?" she asked.

He shook his head, and pursed up his lips negatively.

"I thought not," she said, gaily. "You look like you didn't. Well, I hate— hate —hate—hate smoke. When I go on a ferry-boat, and the air is so nice and cool and different from at home, and seems so clean, I just love it, and then—"

"Some one sits near you and smokes," put in Avery, consolingly.

"Yes, they do; and I just most pray that
he'll fall over and get drownded—but he
never does; and if he asks me if I object to
smoke, I say, "oh! not at all!" and then he
thinks I'm such a nice, sensible girl. Fan
tells 'em right out that she don't like it. It
makes her deadly sick, and the boys all hate
her for it. Her father says it's da—— I was
going to say his cuss word, but I guess I
won't. Anyhow, he says it's all nonsense
and put on. I guess I better go. There is
her father looking for us. Poor Fan'll catch
it when we get home! Good-night. I've
had a lovely time, haven't you?" She
waved her hand. Then she retraced the
step she had taken. "Don't tell that I don't
like tobacco," she said, and started away
laughing. He followed her a few steps.

"How is any fellow to know what you
really do like?" he asked, smiling, "if you
do that way?"

"Fan says nobody wants to know," she
said, slyly. "She says they want to know
that I like what they want me to like, and
think what they think I think." She laughed
again. "And of course I do," she added,

and bowed in mock submission. "Now, Fan
don't. That's where she misses it; and if
she don't — reform," she said, lowering her
voice, as she neared that young lady's
father, "she is going to see trouble that is
trouble. I'll bet a cent on it. Don't you?"
she asked, as she bestowed a bright smile
upon Mr. King.

"Yes," said Avery, and lifting his hat,
turned on his heel and was lost in the
crowd.

"Where's Fan?" inquired that young
lady's father in a tone which indicated that,
as a matter of course, she was up to some
devilment again.

"She got a headache and went home
quite a while ago," said that young lady's
loyal little friend. "She enjoyed it quite a
lot till she did get a headache." As they
neared the street where both lived, Ettie
said: "That man talked to her, and I think
she liked him."

"Humph!" said Mr. King. "I wouldn't
be surprised. She'd be likely to take to a
lunatic. I thought he was about the damned-
est fool I ever saw; didn't you?"

"Yes," said Ettie, laughing, "and I liked him for it."

Mr. King burst into a roar of laughter. "Of course you did! You'd like the devil. You're that easy to please. I wish to the Lord Fan was," and with a hearty "good-night," he left her at her father's door, and crossed the street.

Once outside the garden, Avery drew from his pocket the little pamphlet which his club friend had given him, and ran his finger down the list.

"King, member the — ah, ha! one end of his ward joins mine! 'M-m-m; yes, I see. He is one of the butchers. I suspected as much. Let me see; yes, he votes my ticket, too. If I'm elected we'll be comrades-in-arms, so to speak. I suppose I ought to have told him who I was; but if I'm elected he'll find out soon enough, and if I'm beaten — well, I can't say that I'm anxious to extend the acquaintance." He replaced the book in his pocket as the guard called out, 'Thirty-Fourth Street! 'strain for Arlem!' and left the train, musing as he strolled along. "Yes, Gertrude was quite right —

quite. We fortunate ones have no right to
allow all this sort of thing to go on. We
have no right to leave it entirely to such
men as that to make the laws. I don't care
if the fellows up at the club do guy me.
Gertrude —" He drew from his breast-
pocket a little note, and read it for the tenth
time.

"I am so gratified to hear that you have
accepted the nomination," it said. "You
have the time, and mental and moral equip-
ment to give to the work. Were I a man,
I should not sleep o' nights until some way
was devised to prevent all the terrible poverty and ignorance and brutishness we were
talking about the other day. I went to see
that Spillini family again. I was afraid to
go alone, so I took with me two girls who
are in a sewing class, which is, just now, a
fad at our Church Guild. I thought their
experience with poverty would enable them
to think of a way to get at this case; but it
did not. They appeared to think it was all
right. It seems to me that ignorance and
poverty leave no room for thought, or even
for much feeling. It hurt me like a knife to

have those girls laugh over it after we came out; at least, one of them laughed, and the other seemed scornful. It is not fair to expect more of them, I know, for we expect so little of ourselves. It is thinking of all this that makes me write to tell you how glad I am that you are to represent your district in Albany. Such men are needed, for I know you will work for the poor with the skill of a trained intellect and a sympathetic heart. I am so glad. Sincerely your friend, Gertrude Foster."

Mr. Avery replaced the note in his pocket, and smiled contentedly. "I don't care a great deal what the fellows at the club say," he repeated. "I'm satisfied, if Gertrude—" He had spoken the last few words almost audibly, and the name startled him. He realized for the first time that he had fallen into the habit of thinking of her as Gertrude, and it suddenly flashed upon him that Miss Foster might be a good deal surprised by that fact if she knew it. He fell to wondering if she would also be annoyed. There was a tinge of anxiety in the speculation. Then it occurred to him that the sewing class of the Guild might give an outlet and a chance for a bit of pleasure to that strange girl he had seen at Grady's Pavilion, and he made a little memorandum, and decided to call upon Gertrude and suggest it to her. He fell asleep that night and dreamed of Gertrude Foster, holding out a helping hand to a strange, tall girl, with dissatisfied eyes, and that Ettie Berton was laughing gaily and making everybody comfortable, by asserting that she liked everything exactly as she found it.

VI.

The next evening Avery called upon Gertrude to thank her for her letter, and, incidentally, to tell her of the experience at Grady's Pavilion, and bespeak the good office of the Guild for those two human pawns, who had, somehow, weighed upon his heart.

Avery was not a Churchman himself, but he felt very sure that any Guild which would throw Gertrude Foster's influence about less fortunate girls, would be good, so he gave very little thought to the phase of it which was not wholly related to the personality of the young woman in whose eyes he had grown to feel he must appear well and worthy, if he retained his self-respect. This bar of judgment had come, by unconscious degrees, to be the one before which he tried his own cases for and against himself.

"Would Gertrude like it if she should
know? Would I dislike to have her know
that I did this or felt that?" was now so
constantly a part of his mental processes,
that he had become quite familiar with her
verdicts, which were most often passed —
from his point of view, and in his own mind
— without the knowledge of the girl herself.

He had never talked of love to her, except
in the general and impersonal fashion of
young creatures who are wont to eagerly
discuss the profound perplexities of life
without having come face to face with one
of them. One day they had talked of love
in a cottage. The conversation had been
started by the discussion of a new novel
they had just read, and Avery told her of a
strange fellow whom he knew, who had married against the wishes of his father, and
had been disinherited.

"He lost his grip, somehow," said Avery,
"and went from one disaster into another.
First he lost his place, and the little salary
they had to live on was stopped. It was no
fault of his. It had been in due course of a
business change in the firm he worked for.

He got another, but not so good a situation, but the little debts that had run up while he was idle were a constant drag on him. He never seemed able to catch up. Then his wife's health failed. She needed a change of climate, rare and delicate food, a quiet mind relieved of anxiety, but he could not give her these. His own nerves gave way under the strain, and at last sickness overtook him, and he had to appeal to me for a loan."

It was the letter which his friend had written when in that desperate frame of mind, which Avery read to Gertrude the day they had discussed the novel together. It was a strange, desperate letter, and it had greatly stirred Gertrude. One passage in it had rather shocked her. It was this: "When a fellow is young, and knows little enough of life to accept the fictions of fiction as guides, he talks or thinks about it as 'love in a cottage.' After he has tried it a while, and suffered in heart and soul *because* of his love of those whom he must see day after day handicapped in mind and wrecked in body for the need of larger means, he

begins to speak of it mournfully as 'poverty
with love.' But when that awful day comes,
when sickness or misfortune develops before
his helpless gaze all the horrors of dependence and agony of mind that the future outlook shows him, then it is that the fitting
description comes, and he feels like painting
above the door he dreads to enter — 'hell at
home.' Without the love there would be no
home; without the poverty no hell. Neither
lightens the burdens of the other. Each
multiplies all that is terrible in both."

Gertrude had listened to the letter with a
sad heart. When she did not speak, Avery
felt that he should modify some of its terms
if he would be fair to his absent acquaintance.

"Of course he would have worded it a
little differently if he had known that anyone else would read it. He was desperate.
He had gone through such a succession of
disasters. If anything was going to fall it .
seemed as if he was sure to be under it, so I
don't much wonder at his language after —"

"I don't wonder at it at all," said Gertrude, looking steadily into the fire. "What

seems wonderful, is the facts which his
words portray. I can see that they are
facts; but what I cannot see is—is—"

"How he could express them so raspingly
—so—?" began Avery, but she turned to
him quite frankly surprised.

"Oh, no! Not that. But how can it be
right that it should be so? And if it is not
right, why do not you men who have the
power, do something to straighten things
out? Is this sort of suffering absolutely
necessary in the world?"

It was this talk and its suggestions which
had led Avery to first take seriously into
consideration the proposition that he run for
a seat in the Assembly. It seemed to him
that men like himself, who had both leisure
and convictions, might do some good work
there, and he began to realize that the law-
making of the state was left, for the most
part, in very dangerous hands, and that a
law once passed must inevitably help to
crystalize public opinion in such a way as
to retard freer or better action.

"To think of allowing that class of men
to set the standards about which public

opinion forms and rallies!" he thought, as
the professional politician arose before him,
and his mind was made up. He would be a
candidate. So the night after his experience at Grady's Pavilion he had another
puzzle to lay before Gertrude. When he
entered the hallway he was sorry to hear
voices in the drawing-room. He had hoped
to find Gertrude and her mother alone. His
first impulse was to leave his card and call
at another time, but the servant, recognizing his hesitation, ventured a bit of information.

"Excuse me, Mr. Avery, but I don't think
they will be here long. It's a couple of —
They — "

" Thank you, James. Are they not friends
of Miss Gertrude?"

James smiled in a manner which dis-
played a large capacity for pity.

" Well, sir, I shouldn't say they was exactly friends. No, sir, ner yet callers, sir.
They're some of them Guilders."

Avery could not guess what Gertrude
would have gilders in the drawing-room for
at that hour, but decided to enter. "Mr.

Avery;" said James, in his most formal and
perfunctory fashion, as he drew back the
portiere and announced the new arrival. No
one would have dreamed from the stolid
front presented by the liveried functionary,
that he had just exchanged confidences with
the guest.

"Let me introduce my friends to you, Mr.
Avery," began Gertrude, and two figures
arose, and from one came a gay little laugh,
a mock courtesy, and "Law me! It's him!
Well, if this don't beat the Dutch!"

She extended her hand to him and laughed
again. "We didn't shake hands last night,
but now's we're regul'rly interduced I guess
we will," she added.

Avery took her hand, and then offered
his to her companion, and bowed and smiled
again.

"Really, I shall begin to grow supersti-
tious," he said, in an explanatory tone to
Gertrude. "I came here to-night to see if
I could arrange to have you three young
ladies meet; to learn if there was a chance
at the Guild to — "

"Oh," smiled Gertrude, beginning to

grasp the situation. "How very nice! But
these two are my star girls at the Guild
now. We were just arranging some work
for next week, but —"

"Yas, she wants to go down to that Spillini hole agin," broke in Ettie Berton, and
Francis King glanced suspiciously from
Gertrude to Avery. She wondered just
what these two were thinking. She felt
very uncomfortable and wished that he had
not come in. She had not spoken since
Avery entered, and he realized her discom-
fort.

"You treated us pretty shabbily last
night, Miss King," he said, smiling, and
then he turned to Gertrude. "She left me
in the middle of a remark. We met at
Grady's Pavilion, and if I'm elected, I learn
that the fathers of both of these young
ladies will be my companions-in-arms in the
Assembly. They —" In spite of herself,
Gertrude's face showed her surprise, but
Ettie Berton broke in with a gay laugh.

"Are you in politics? Law me! I'd
never a believed it. I don't see how you're
agoin' to get on unless you get a —"

She realized that her remark was going to indicate a belief in certain incapacity in him, and she took another cue.

"My pa says nobody hardly can't get on in politics by himself. You see my pa is a sort of a starter for Fan's pa in politics, 're else he'd never got on in the world. Fan's pa backs him, and he starts things that her pa wants started."

Francis moved uneasily, and Gertrude said: "That is natural enough since they were friends here, and, I think you told me, were in business together, didn't you?"

Ettie laughed, and clapped her hands gaily. "That's good! In business together! Oh, Lord, I'll tell pa that. He'll roar. Why, pa is a prerofessional starter. He ain't in business with no particular one only jest while the startin's done."

The girl appeared to think that Avery and Gertrude were quite familiar with professional starters, and she rattled on gaily.

"I thought I'd die the time he started them butcher shops for Fan's pa, though. He hadn't never learnt the difference between a rib roast 'n a soup bone, 'n he had

to keep a printed paper hung up inside o'
the ice chest so's he'd know which kind of a
piece he got out to sell; but he talked so
nice an' smooth all the time he *was* a gettin'
it out, an' tole each customer that the piece
they asked fer was the ' choicest part of the
animal,' but that mighty few folks had sense
enough to know it — oh, it was funny! I
used to get where I could hear him, and jest
die a laughin'. He'd sell the best in the
shop for ten cents a pound, an' he'd cut it
which ever way they ast him to, an' make
heavy weight. His price list was a holy
show, but he jest scooped in all the trade
around there in no time, an' the other shops
had to move. Then you ought t' a seen
Fan's pa come in there an' brace things up!
Whew!" She laughed delightedly, and
Francis's face flushed.

"He braced prices up so stiff that some o'
the customers left, but most of 'em stayed
rather'n hunt up a new place to start books
in. Pa, he'd started credit books with *all*
of 'em.

Pa, he was in the back room the first day
Fan's pa and the new clerk took the shop,

after pa got it good'n started. Him an'
me most died laughin' at the kickin' o' the
people. Every last one of 'em ast fer pa to
wait on 'em, but Fan's pa he told 'em that
he'd bankrupted hisself and had t' sell out
to him. Pa said he wisht he had somethin'
to bankrupt on. But, law, he'll never make
no money. He ain't built that way. He's
a tip-top perfessional starter tho', ain't he,
Fan?" she concluded with a gleeful reminis-
cent grimace at her friend. Francis shifted
her position awkwardly, and tried to feel
that everything was quite as it should be in
good society, and Gertrude made a little
attempt to divert the conversation to affairs
of the Guild, but Ettie Berton, who appeared to look upon her father as a huge
joke, and to feel herself most at home in
discussing him, broke in again: —

"But the time he started the 'Stable fer
Business Horses,' was the funniest yet,"
and she laughed until her eyes filled with
tears, and she dried them with the lower
part of the palms of her hands, rubbing
them red.

"The boss told him not to take anything

but business horses. What he meant was, to be sure not to let in any fancy high-steppers, fer fear they'd get hurt or sick, an' he'd have trouble about 'em. Well, pa didn't understand at first, an' he wouldn't take no mules, an' most all the business horses around there *was* mules, an' when drivers 'd ask him why he wouldn't feed 'em 'er take 'em in, he jest had t' fix up the funniest stories y' ever heard. He tole one man that he hadn't laid in the kind o' feed mules eat, n' the man told him he was the biggest fool to talk he ever see. The mule-man he — "

Francis King had arisen, and started awkwardly toward Gertrude, with her hand extended.

" I think we ought to go," she said, uneasily, her large eyes burning with mortification, and an oppressed sense of being at a disadvantage.

" So soon?" said Gertrude, smiling as she took her hand, and laid her other arm about the shoulders of Ettie, who had hastened to place herself in the group. " I was so entertained that I did not realize that perhaps

you ought to go before it grows late — oh,"
glancing at a tiny watch in her bracelet, "it
is late — too late for you to go way down
there alone. I will send James, or — "

"Allow me the pleasure, will you not?"
asked Avery, bowing first to Gertrude, and
then toward Francis, and Gertrude said: —

"Oh, thank you, if — " but Ettie clapped
her hands in glee.

"Well, that's too rich! Just as if we
didn't go around by ourselves all the time,
and — Lord! pa says if anybody carries me
off he'd only go as far as the lamp-post, and
drop me as soon as the light struck me!
Now Fan's pretty, but — " she laughed, and
made clawing movements in the air. "Nobody 'll get away with Queen Fan 's long 's
she's got finger-nails 'n teeth." She snapped
her pretty little white teeth together with
mock viciousness, and laughed again. "I'd
just pity the fellow that tried any tomfool-
ery with Queen Fan. He'd wish he'd died
young!"

They all laughed a bit at this sally, and
Avery said he did not want Miss King to be
forced to extremities in self-protection while

he was able to relieve her of the necessity.

When James closed the door behind the laughing group, he glanced at Miss Gertrude to see what she thought of it, but he remarked to Susan later on, that "Miss Gertrude looked as if she was born 'n brought up that way herself. She didn't show no amusement ner no sarcasm in her face. An' as fer Mr. Avery, it was nothing short of astonishing, to see him offer his arms to those two Guilders as they started down the avenue."

And Susan ventured it as her present belief, that if Gertrude's father once caught any of her Guilders around, he'd "make short work of the whole business. She ought 't be ashamed o' herself, so she ought. Ketch *me*, if I was in her shoes, a consortin' with —"

"Anybody but me, Susie," put in the devoted James; but alas, for him, the stiff, unyielding hooked joint of his injured finger came first in contact with the wrist of the fair Susan as he essayed to clasp her hand, and she evaded the grasp and flung out of

the room with a shiver. "Keep that old
twisted base ball bat off o' me!" I—"

"Oh, Susie!" said James, dolefully, to
himself, as he slowly surrounded the offending member with the folds of his handkerchief, which gave it the appearance of being
in hospital. "Oh, Susie! how kin you?"

When John Martin, on his way, intending
to drop in for the last act of the opera,
passed Gertrude's door just in time to see
Avery and the two girls come down the
steps, his lip curled a bit, and his heart per-
formed that strange feat which loving hearts
have achieved in all the ages past, in spite
of reason and of natural impulses of kindness. It took on a distinctly hard feeling
towards Avery, and this feeling was not
unmixed with resentment. "How dare he
take girls like that to her house? I was a
fool to take her to the Spillinis, but I'd
never be idiot enough to take that type of
girl to *her* house. Avery's political freak
has dulled his sense of propriety."

Mr. Martin wondered vaguely if he ought
not to say something to Gertrude's father,
and then he thought it might possibly be

better to touch lightly upon it himself in talking to her.

He had heard some gossip at the opera and in the club, which indicated that society did not approve altogether of some of the things Gertrude had recently said and done; but that it smiled approvingly at what it believed to be as good as an engagement between the young lady and Selden Avery. Martin ground his teeth now as he thought of it, and glanced again at the retreating forms of Avery and the two girls.

"It was that visit to the Spillinis, and the revelations of life which it gave her, that is to blame for it all," he groaned. "I was an accursed fool — an accursed fool!"

That night Gertrude lay thinking how charmingly Selden Avery had met the situation, and how well he had helped carry it off with Ettie and Francis. "He seemed to look at it all just as I do," she thought. I felt that I knew just what he was thinking, and he certainly guessed that I wanted him to see them home, exactly as if they had been girls of our own set. Poor little Ettie! I wonder what we can do with, or for, such

as she? She is so hopelessly — happy and
ignorant." Then she fell asleep, and
dreamed of rescuing Ettie from the fangs
of a maddened dog, and Francis stood by
and looked scornfully at Gertrude's lacer-
ated hands, and then pointed to her little
friend's mangled body and the smile upon
her dead lips.

"She never knew what hurt her, and she
teased the dog to begin with," she said.
"You are maimed for life, and may go mad,
just trying to help her — and she never
knew and she never cared." Gertrude's
dream had strayed and wandered into vaga-
ries without form or outline, and in the
morning nothing of it was left but an unrea-
sonably heavy heart, and a restless desire to
do — she knew not what.

VII.

When Avery took his seat in the Assembly he learned that Ettie Berton's father had been true to his calling. He still might be described as a professional starter. Any bill which was in need of some one to either introduce or offer a speech in its favor, found in John Berton an ever-ready champion.

Not that he either understood or believed in all the bills he presented or advocated. Belief and understanding were not for sale; nor, indeed, were they always very much within his own grasp. He was in the Legislature to promote, or start, such measures as stood in need of his peculiar abilities. This was very soon understood, and many a bill which other men feared or hesitated to present, found its way to him and through him to a reading. For a while Avery watched this process with amusement. He wrote to Gertrude, from time to time, some

very humorous letters about it; but finally,
one day a letter came which so bitterly de-
nounced both King and Berton, that Gertrude wondered what could have wrought
the sudden change.

"He has introduced a bill which is now
before my committee," he wrote, "that
passes all belief. It is infamous beyond
words to express, and, to my dismay, it finds
many advocates beside King and Berton.
That a conscienceless embruted inmate of
an opium dive in Mott Street might acknowledge to himself in the dark, and when
he was alone, that he could advocate such
a measure, seems to me possible; but
men who are in one sense reputable,
who — many of them — look upon themselves as respectable; men who are fathers
of girls and brothers of women, could even
consider such a bill, I would not have believed possible, and yet, I am ashamed to
say that I learn now for the first time, that
our state is not the only one where similar
measures have not only found advocates,
but where there were enough moral lepers
with voting power to establish such legisla-

tion. It makes me heartsick and desperate.
I am ashamed of the human race. I am
doubly ashamed that it is to my sex such
infamous laws are due.

"You were right, my dear Miss Gertrude;
you were right. It is outrageous that we
allow mere conscienceless politicians to legislate for respectable people, and yet my
position here is neither pleasant, nor will it, I
fear, be half so profitable as you hope — as
I hoped, before I came and learned all I now
know. But, believe me, I shall vote on
every bill and make every speech, with your
face before me, and as if I were making that
particular law to apply particularly to you."

Gertrude smiled as she re-read that part
of his letter.

She wondered what awful bill Ettie's
father had presented. She had never before
thought that a legislator might strive to
enact worse laws than he already found in
the statute books. She had thought most
of the trouble was that they did not take
the time and energy to repeal old, bad laws
that had come to us from an ignorant or
brutal past.

It struck her as a good idea, that a man should never vote on a measure that he did not feel he was making a rule of action to apply to the woman for whom he cared most; she knew now that she was that woman for Selden Avery. He had told her that the night he came to bring the news that he was elected. It had been told in a strangely simple way.

Her father and mother had laughingly congratulated him upon his election, and Mr. Foster had added, banteringly: "If one may congratulate a man upon taking a descent like that."

Gertrude had held one of her father's hands in her own, and tried by gentle pressure to check him. Her father laughed, and added: "The little woman here is trying to head me off. She appears to think—"

"Papa," said Gertrude, extending her other hand to Avery, "I do think that Mr. Avery is to be congratulated that he has the splendid courage to try to do something distinctly useful for other people, than simply for the few of us who are outside or above most of the horrors of life. I do—"

Avery suddenly lifted her hand to his lips, and his eyes told the rest. "Mr. Foster," he said, still holding the girl's hand, and blushing painfully, "there can never be but one horror in the world too awful for me to face, and that would be to lose the full respect and confidence of your daughter. I know I have those now, and for the rest—" He glanced again at Gertrude. She was pale, and she was looking with an appeal in her eyes to her mother.

Mrs Foster moved a step nearer, and put her arm about the girl. "For the rest, Mr. Avery, for the rest—later on, later on," she said, kindly. "Gertrude has traveled very fast these past few months, but she is her mother's girl yet." Then she smiled kindly, and added: "Gertrude has set a terrible standard for the man she will care for. I tremble for him and I tremble for her."

"Tut, tut," said her father, "there are no standards in love—none whatever. Love has its own way, and standards crumble—"

"In the past, perhaps. But in the future—" began his wife.

"In the future," said Gertrude, as she drew nearer to her mother, "In the future they may not need to crumble, because,—because—" Her eyes met Avery's, and fell. She saw that his muscles were tense, and his face was unhappy.

"Because men will be great enough and true enough to rise to the ideals, and not need to crumble the ideals to bring them to their level."

Avery bent forward and grasped her hand that was within her mother's.

"Thank you," he said, tremulously. "Thank you, oh, darling! and the rest can wait," he said, to Mrs. Foster, and dropping both hands, he left the room and the house.

Gertrude ran up-stairs and locked her door.

Mr. Foster turned to his wife with a half amused, half vexed face. "Well, this is a pretty kettle of fish. What's to become of Martin, I'd like to know?"

"John Martin has never had a ghost of a chance at any time — never," said his wife, slowly trailing her gown over the rug, and dragging with it a small stand that had caught its carved claw in the lace. It toppled and fell with a crash. The beautiful vase it had held was in fragments.

"Oh, Katharine!" exclaimed her husband, springing forward to disengage her lace. "Oh, it is too bad, isn't it?"

And Katherine Foster burst into tears, and with her arms suddenly thrown about her husband's neck she sobbed: "Oh, yes, it is too bad! It is too bad!" But it did not seem possible to her husband that the broken vase could have so affected her, and surely no better match could be asked for Gertrude. It could not be that. He was deeply perplexed, and Katherine Foster, with a searching look in her face, kissed him sadly as one might kiss the dead, and went to her daughter's room.

She tapped lightly and then said, "It is I, daughter."

The girl opened the door and as quickly closed and locked it. Instantly their arms were around each other and both were close to tears.

"Don't try to talk, darling," whispered Mrs. Foster, as they sat down upon the couch. "Don't try to talk. I understand better than you do yet, and oh, Gertrude, your mother loves you!"

"Yes, mamma" said the girl, hoarsely. "Dear little mamma—poor little mamma, we all love you;" and Mrs. Foster sighed.

VIII.

The day Gertrude received Avery's letter about bill number 408, she asked her father what the bill was about. He looked at her in surprise, and then at his wife. "I don't know anything about it, child," he said; "Why?"

Gertrude drew from her pocket Avery's letter and read that part of it. Her father's face clouded.

"What business has he to worry you with his dirty political work? I infer from what he says that it is a bill that I've only heard mentioned once or twice. The sort of thing they do in secret sessions and keep from the newspapers in the main. That is, they are only barely named in the paper and under a number or heading which people don't understand. I'm disgusted with Avery — perfectly!"

Gertrude was surprised, but with that

ignorance and absolute sincerity of youth, she appealed to her mother.

"Mamma, do you see any reason why, from that letter, papa should be vexed with Mr. Avery? It seemed to me to have just the right tone; but I am sorry he did not tell me just what the bill is."

"You let me catch him telling you, if it's what I think it is," retorted her father, rather hotly. "It's not fit for your ears. Good women have no business with such knowledge and —"

Mrs. Foster held up a warning finger to her daughter, but the girl had not been convinced.

"Don't good men know such things, papa? Don't such bills deal with people in a way which will touch women, too? I can't see why you put it that way. If a bill is to be passed into a law, and it is of so vile a nature as you say and as this letter indicates, in whose interest is it to be silent or ignorant? Do you want such a bill passed? Would mamma or I?"

Her father laughed, and rose from the table. "It is in the interest of nothing

good. No, I should say if you or your
mother, or any other respectable mother
at all, were in the Legislature, no such
bill would have a ghost of a chance; but —"

Gertrude's eyes were fixed upon her
father. They were very wide open and
perplexed.

"Then it can be only in the interest of
the vilest and lowest of the race that good
men keep silent, and prefer to have good
women ignorant and helpless in such—"
she began; but her father turned at the
door and said, nervously and almost sharply,
"Gertrude, if Avery has no more sense
than to start you thinking about such
things, I advise you to cut his acquaintance.
Such topics are not fit for women; I am perfectly disgusted with—"

As he was passing out of the dining-
room, John Martin entered the street door
and faced him. "Hello, Martin! Glad to
see you! The ladies are still at luncheon;
won't you come right in here and join them
in a cup of chocolate?"

He was heartily glad of the interruption,

and felt that it was very timely indeed that
Mr. Martin had dropped in.

"No, I can't take off my top-coat. Get
yours. I want you to join me in a spin in
the park. I've got that new filly outside."
Mr. Foster ran up-stairs to get ready for the
drive, and the ladies insisted that a cup of
hot chocolate was the very thing to prepare
Mr. Martin for the nipping air. He was a
trifle ill at ease. He wanted to speak of
Selden Avery, and he feared if he did so
that he would say the wrong thing. He
had come to-day, partly to have a talk with
his friend Foster about certain gossip he
had heard. Fate took the reins.

In rising, Gertrude had dropped Avery's
letter. John Martin was the first to see it.
He laughingly offered it to her with the
query: "Do you sow your love letters about
that way, Miss Gertrude?"

"Gertrude's love letters take the form of
political speeches just now, and bills and
committee reports and the like," laughed
her mother. Her father was just showing
his teeth over that one. He thinks women
have no—"

"Mr. Martin, tell me truly," broke in the girl, "tell me truly, don't you think that we are all equally interested in having only good laws made? And don't you think if a proposed measure is too bad for good women even to be told what it is, that it is bad enough for all good people to protest against?"

"How are they going to protest if they don't know what it is?" laughed Martin. "Well, Miss Gertrude, I believe that is the first time I ever suspected you to be of Celtic blood. But what dreadful measure is Avery advocating now?" he smiled. "Really, I shouldn't have believed it of Avery!"

"What!" exclaimed Mr. Foster, entering with his top-coat buttoned to the chin, and his driving-hat in hand. Gertrude still held the letter. "No, nor should I have believed it of Avery. It was an outrageous thing for him to do. What business has Gertrude or Katherine with his disgusting old bills. Just before you came in I advised Gertrude to cut him entirely, and —"

Mrs. Foster was trying to indicate to her

husband that he was off the track, and that
Mr. Martin did not understand him; but he
had the bit in his teeth and went on. "You
agree with me now, don't you? What do
you think of his mentioning such things to
Gertrude?" He reached over and took the
letter from his daughter's hand, and read a
part of the obnoxious paragraph.

John Martin's face was a study. He
glanced at the two ladies, and then fixed
his eyes upon Gertrude's father.

"Good Gad!" he said, slowly and almost
below his breath. "If I were in your place
I should shoot him. The infamous —" He
checked himself, and the two men withdrew.
Gertrude and her mother waved at them
from the window, and then the girl said:
"I intend to know what that bill is. What
right have men to make laws that they
themselves believe are too infamous for
good women even to know about? Don't
you believe if all laws or bills had to be
openly discussed before and with women, it
would be better, mamma? I do."

Her mother's cheek was against the cold
glass of the window. She was watching

the receding forms. Presently she turned
slowly to her daughter and said, in a trembling tone: —

"Such bills as this one," she drew a small
printed slip from her bosom and handed it
to Gertrude, "such bills as that would never
be dreamed of by men if they knew they
must pass the discussion of a pure girl or a
mother—never! Their only chance is
secret session, and the fact that even men
like your—like Mr. Martin and— and —"
she was going to say "your father," but the
girl pressed her hand and she did not.
"That even such as they—for what reason
heaven only knows—think they are serving
the best interests of the women they love by
a silence which fosters and breeds just such
measures as—"

Gertrude was reading the queer, blind
phraseology of the bill. Katherine had
watched her daughter's face as she talked,
and now the girl's lips were moving and she
read audibly: "be, and is hereby enacted,
that henceforth the legal age in the state of
New York whereat a female may give con-

sent to the violation of her own person shall be reduced to ten years."

Gertrude dropped the paper in her lap and looked up like a frightened, hunted creature. "Great God!" she exclaimed, with an intensity born of a sudden revelation. "Great God! and they call themselves men! And other men keep silence—furnish all the soil and nurture for infamy like that! Those who keep silence are as guilty as the rest! Those who try to prevent women from knowing—oh, mamma!" Her eyes were intense. She sprang to her feet; "and John Martin, who thinks he loves *me* is one of those men! Knowing such a bill as that is pending, his indignation is aroused, not at the bill, not at the men who try to smuggle it through, not at the awful thing it implies, but that so strict a silence is not kept that such as *we* may not know of it! He blames Selden Avery for coming to me—to us—with his splendid chivalry, and sharing with us his horror, making us the confidants of that inner conscience which sees, in the intended victims of this awful bill, his little sisters and yours and mine!" There were indignant tears in her eyes. She closed them, and her white lips were drawn tense. Presently she asked, without opening her eyes: "Mamma, do you suppose if you, instead of Mr. Avery, were chairman of that committee, that such a bill as that would ever have been presented? Do you suppose, if any mother on earth held the veto power, that such a bill would ever disgrace a statute book? Are there enough men, even of a class who generally go to the Legislature, who, in spite of their fatherhood, in spite of the fact that they have little sisters, are such beasts as to pass a bill like that? A ten-year-old girl! A mere baby! And—oh, mamma! it is too hideous to believe, even of—such a bill could never pass. Never on earth! Surely, Ettie Berton, poor little thing, has the only father living who is capable of that!"

Mrs. Foster opened her lips to say that several states already had the law, and that one had placed the age at seven; but she checked herself. Her daughter's excitement was so great, she decided to wait. The experience of the past few months had awakened the fire in the nature of this strong daughter of hers. She had seen the cool, steady, previously indifferent, well-poised girl stirred to the very depths of her nature over the awful conditions of poverty, ignorance, and vice she had, for the first time, learned to know. Gertrude had become a regular student of some of the problems of life, and she had carried her studies into practical investigation. It had grown to be no new thing for her to take Francis, or Ettie, or both, when she went on these errands, and the study of their points of view—of the effect of it all upon their ignorance-soaked minds, had been one of the most touching things to her. Their imaginations were so stunted—so embryonic, so undeveloped that they saw no better way. To them, ignorance, poverty, squalor, and vice were a necessary part of life. Wealth, comfort, happiness, ambition were, naturally and rightly, perquisites, some way, some how, of the few.

"God rules, and all is as he wishes it or it would not be that way," sagely remarked Francis King, one day. It had startled Gertrude. Her philosophy, her observation, her

reason, and her religion were in a state of
conflict just then. She had alway supposed
that she was an Episcopalian with all that
this implied. She was beginning to doubt
it at times.

Mrs. Foster looked at her daughter now,
as she sat there flushed and excited. She
wondered what would come of it all. She
had always studied this daughter of hers,
and tried to follow the girl's moods. Now
she thought she would cut across them.
"Gertrude, you may put that bill with your
letter. Mr. Avery mailed it to me. Of
course he meant that I should show it to you
if I thought best. I did think best, but now
—but—I don't want you to excite yourself
too—" She broke off suddenly. Her
daughter's eyes were upon her in surprise.
Mrs. Foster laughed a little nervously, and
kissed the girl's hand as it lay in her own.
"It seems rather droll for your gay little
mother to caution you against losing control
of yourself, doesn't it?" she asked. "You
who were always all balance wheel, as your
father says. But—"

"Mamma, don't you think Mr. Avery did

perfectly right to send me that letter and
this to you?" broke in Gertrude, as if she
had not heard the admonition of her mother,
and had followed her own thoughts from
some more distant point.

"Perfectly," said her mother. "He was
evidently deeply disturbed by the bill. He
felt that you were, and should be, his con-
fidant. He simply did not dream of hiding
it from you, I believe. It was the sponta-
neous act of one who so loves you that his
whole life—all of that which moves him
greatly—must, as a matter of course, be open
to you. I thought that all out when the bill
came addressed to me. He—" The girl
kissed her in silence.

"You have such splendid self-respect,
Gertrude. Most of us—most women—
have none. We do not expect, do not
demand, the least respect that is real from
men. They have no respect for our opinions,
and so upon all the real and important things
of life, they hold out to us the sham of
silence as more respectful than candor.
And we—most of us—are weak enough to
say we like it. Most of us—"

Gertrude slipped down upon a cushion at the feet of her mother, and put her young, strong arms about the supple waist. She had of late read from time to time so much of the unrest and scorn back of the gay and compliant face of her mother. "Mamma, my real mamma," she said, softly, "I am so sorry for papa that he should have missed so much, so much that might have been his! A mental comrade like you—"

"Men of your father's generation did not want mental comrades in their wives, Gertrude. They—"

"A telegram, Miss Gertrude," said James, drawing aside the portiere.

"The bill has been rushed through. Passed. Nineteen majority. Avery." Gertrude read it and handed it to her mother, and both women sat as if stunned by a blow.

IX.

At the close of the Legislature, John
Berton, professional starter, and his friend
and ally, the father of Francis King, had
returned to the city. Francis had grown,
so her father thought, more handsome and
less agreeable than ever. Her eyes were
more dissatisfied, and she was, if possible,
less pliant. She and Ettie Berton were
working now in a store, and Francis said
that she did not like it at all. The money
she liked. It helped her to dress more as
she wished, and then it had always cut
Francis to the quick to be compelled to ask
her father for money whenever she needed
it, even for car fare.

She had lied a good many times. Her
whole nature rebelled against lying, but
even this was easier to her than the status
of dependence and beggary, so she had lied
often about the price of shoes, or of a hat

or dress, that there might be a trifle left
over as a margin for her use in other ways.
Her father was not unusually hard with her
about money, only that he demanded a strict
accounting before he gave it to her.

"What in thunder do you want of
money?" he would ask, more as a matter
of habit than anything else. "How much
'll it take? Humph! Well, I guess you'll
have to have it, but—" and so the ungra-
cious manner of giving angered and humiliated her.

"Pa, give me ten cents; I want it fer car
fare. Thanks. Now fork over six dollars;
I got to get a dress after the car gets me to
the store," was Ettie Berton's method. Her
father would pretend not to have the money,
and she would laugh and proceed to rifle his
pockets. The scuffle would usually end in
the girl getting more than she asked for,
and was no unpleasant experience to her,
and it appeared to amuse her father greatly.
It was not, therefore, the same motive which
actuated the two when they decided to try
their fortunes as shop girls. The desire to
be with Francis, to be where others were,

for the sight and touch of the pretty things, for new faces and for mild excitement, were moving causes with Ettie Berton. The money she liked, too; but if she could have had the place without the money or the money without the place, her choice would have been soon made. She would stay at the store. That she was a general favorite was a matter of course. She would do anything for the other girls, and the floor-walkers and clerks found her always obedient and gaily willing to accept extra burdens or to change places. For some time past, however, she had been on a different floor from the one where Francis presided over a trimming counter, and the girls saw little of each other, except on their way to and from the store.

At last this changed too, for Francis was obliged to remain to see that the stock of her department was properly put away. At first Ettie waited for her, but later on she had fallen into the habit of going with a child nearer her own age, a little cash girl. Ettie was barely fourteen, and her new friend a year or two younger. At last

Francis King found that the motherless child had invited her new friends home with her, and had gone with them to their homes.

As spring came on, Ettie went one Sunday to Coney Island, and did not tell Francis until afterward. She said that she had had a lovely time, but she appeared rather disinclined to talk about it. At the Guild one Wednesday evening, after the class began again in the fall, Francis King told Gertrude this, and asked her advice. She said: "It's none o' my business, and she don't like me much any more, but I thought maybe I had ought to tell you, for — for — since I been in the store, I've learnt a good deal about — about things; an' Ettie she don't seem to learn much of anything."

"Is Ettie still living at her cousin's?" asked Gertrude.

"Yes," said Francis, scornfully, "but she 'bout as well be livin' by herself. Her cousin's always just gaddin' 'round tryin' t' get married. I never did see such an awful fool. Before Et's pa went to the Legislature, we all did think he was goin' t' marry her, but now — "

"Legislative honors have turned his head, have they?" smiled Gertrude, intent on her own thoughts in another direction. She was not, therefore, prepared for the sudden fling of temper in the strange girl beside her.

"Yes, it has; 'n if it don't turn some other way before long, I'll break his neck for him. *I* ain't marryin' a widower if I do like Ettie."

In spite of herself, Gertrude started a little. She looked at Francis quite steadily for a moment, and then said: "Could you and Ettie come to my house and spend the day next Sunday? I'm glad you told me of Ettie's — of — about the change in her manner toward you."

"Don't let on that I told you anything," said Francis, as they parted.

Since they had been in the store they had not gone regularly to the weekly evening Guild meetings, and Gertrude had seen less of them. She was surprised, however, on the following Sunday, to see the strange, mysterious change in Ettie. A part of her frank, open, childish manner was gone, and yet nothing more mature had taken its place. There would be flashes of her usual manner, but long silences, quite foreign to the child, would follow. At the dinner table she grew deadly ill, and had to be taken up stairs. Gertrude tucked a soft cover about her on the couch in her own room, and gave her smelling salts and a trifle of wine. The child drank the wine but began to cry.

"Oh, don't cry, Ettie," said Gertrude, stroking her hair gently. "You'll be over it in a little while. I think our dining-room is much warmer than yours, and it was very hot to-day. Then your trying to eat the olives when you don't like them, might easily make you sick. You'll be all right after a little I'm sure. Don't cry."

"That's the same kind of wine I had that day at Coney Island," she said, and Gertrude thought how irrelevant the remark was, and how purely of physical origin were the tears of such a child.

"Would you like a little more?" asked Gertrude, smiling.

Ettie shivered, and closed her eyes.

"No; I don't like it. I guess it ain't
polite to say so, but — Oh, of course *maybe*
I'd like it if I was well, but it made me sick
that time, an' so I don't like it now when I
am sick." She laughed in a childish way,
and then she drew Gertrude's face down
near her own. "Say, I'll tell you the solemn
truth. It made me tight that day. He told
me so afterwards, n' I guess it did."

Here was a revelation, indeed. Gertrude
stroked the fluffy hair, gently. She was
trying to think of just the right thing to
say. It was growing dark in the room.
Ettie reached up again and drew Gertrude's
face down.

"Say," she whispered, "you won't be mad
at me for that, will you? He told me I
wasn't to blab to anybody; but it always
seems as if you wouldn't be mad at me, and"
— she began to weep again.

"Don't cry," said Gertrude, again, gently.
"Of course I am not angry with you. I am
sorry it happened, but — Ettie, who is *he?*"

Ettie sobbed on, and held her arms close
about Gertrude's neck. Again the older
girl said, with lips close to the child's ear:

"Don't you think it would be better to tell me who ' he ' is? Is he so young as to not know better than to advise you that way, dear?"

"He's forty," sobbed Ettie, "an' he's rich, an' he's got a girl of his own as big as me. I saw her one day in the store. He's the cashier."

Gertrude shivered, and the child felt the movement.

"Don't you ever, ever tell," she panted, " or he'll kill me — and so would pa."

"Oh, he would, would he?" exclaimed Francis, who had stolen silently into the room and had stood unobserved in the darkness. "The cashier! the mean devil! I always hated his beady eyes, and he tried his games on me! But I'll kill him before he shall go — do you any real harm, Ettie! I will! I will! Why didn't you tell me? I watched for a while and then I thought — I thought he had given it up. Oh, Ettie, Ettie!" The tall form of the girl seemed to rise even higher in the darkness, and one could feel the fire of her great eyes. Her hands were clenched and her muscles tense.

Ettie was sobbing anew, and Gertrude, holding her hand, was stroking the moist forehead and trying to quiet her.

"Oh, Fan! Oh, Fan! I didn't want you to know," sobbed the child, with pauses between her words. "He said nobody needn't ever know if I'd do just's he told me. He said — but when pa came home I was so scared, an' I'm sick most all the time, an' — an', oh, if I wasn't so awful afraid to die I'd wisht I *was* dead!"

"Dead!" gasped Francis, grasping Ettie's wrist and pulling her hand from her face in a frenzy of the new light that was dawning upon her half-dazed but intensely stimulated mental faculties. She half pulled the smaller girl to her feet.

"Dead! Ettie Berton, you tell me the God's truth or I'll tear him to pieces right in the store. You tell me the God's truth! has he — done anything awful to you?" A young tiger could not have seemed more savage, and Ettie clung with her other arm to Gertrude.

"No! No! No!" she shrieked, and struggled to free herself from the clutch upon

her wrist. Then with the pathetic superstition and ignorance of her type: "Cross
my heart! Hope I may die!" she added, and
as Francis relaxed her grasp upon the wrist,
Ettie fell in an unconscious little heap upon
the floor.

Francis was upon her knees beside her in
an instant, and Gertrude was about to ring
for a light and for her mother when Francis
moaned: "Oh, send for a doctor, quick.
Send for a doctor! She was lying and she
crossed her heart. She will die! She will
die!"

X.

But Ettie Berton did not die.   Perhaps it
would have been quite as well for her if she
had died before the impotent and frantic
rage of her father had still further darkened
the pathetically appealing, love-hungry little
heart, whose every beat had been a throb-
bing, eager desire to be liked, to please, to
acquiesce; to the end that she should escape
blame, that she might sail on the smooth
and pleasant sea of general praise and
approval.

Alas, the temperament which had brought
her the dangerous stimulus of praise, for
self-effacement, had joined hands with opportunity to wreck the child's life — and no
one was more bitter in his denunciation than
her father's friend and her aforetime admirer — Representative King.   "If she was
a daughter o' mine I'd kill her," he repeated
to his own household day after day.   "She

sh'd never darken *my* door agin. That's
mighty certain. It made me mad the other
day to hear Berton talk about takin' her
back home. The old fool! What does he
want of her? An' what kind of an example's that I'd like t' know t' set t' decent
girls? I told him right then an' there if he
let his soft heart do him that a'way I was
done with him for good an' all, n' if I ketch
you a goin' up there t' see her agin, you can
just stay away from here, that's all!" This
last had been to Francis, and Francis had
shut her teeth together very hard, and the
glitter in her eyes might have indicated to a
wiser man that it was not chiefly because of
his presence there that this daughter cared
to return to her home after her clandestine
visits to Ettie Berton. A wiser man, too,
might have guessed that the prohibition
would not prohibit, and that poor little Ettie
Berton would not be deserted by her loyal
friend because of his displeasure.

"I have told her that she may live with
us by and by," said Gertrude to Seldon
Avery one afternoon; "but that is no solution of the problem. And besides, it is her

father's duty to care for her and to do it
without hurting the child's feelings, too.
Can't you go to him and have a talk with
him? You say he seems a kindhearted,
well-meaning, easily-led man. Beside, he
has no right to blame her. He has done
more than any one else in this state to make
the path of the cashier easy and smooth. If
it were not for poor little Ettie I should be
heartily glad of it all — of the lesson for
him. Can't you go to him and to that Mr.
King and make them see the infamy of their
work, and force them to undo it? Can't
you? Is there no way?"

Avery had gone. He argued in vain.
"Why do you blame the cashier," he had said
to Berton. "He has committed no legal
offence. Our laws say he has done no
wrong. Then why blame him? Why blame
Ettie? She is a mere yielding, impulsive
child, and, surely, if he has done no wrong
she has not. If—"

"Now look a-here, Mr. Avery," said John
Berton, hotly, "I know what you're a-hittin'
at an' you can jest save your breath. I
didn't help pass that law t' apply to *my* girl,

n' you know it damned well. I ain't in no mood just now t' have you throw it up to me that she was about the first one it ketched, neather. How was I a-goin' to know that? That there bill wasn't intended t' apply t' *my* girl, I tell you. An' then she hadn't ought to a said she went with him willin'ly, either. If she hadn't a said that we could a peppered him, but as it is he's all right, an —"

"That is what the law contemplates, isn't it?—for other girls, of course, not for yours," began Avery, whose natural impulses of kindness and generosity he was holding back.

"Now you hold on!" exclaimed Berton, feebly groping about for a reply. "You know I never got up that bill. You know mighty well the man that got it up an' come there an' lobbied for it, was one o' *your* own kind — a silk stocking.

"You know I only started it 'n' sort o' fathered it for *him*. I ain't no more to blame than the others. Go 'n talk t' them. I've had my dose. Go 'n talk t' King. He says yet that it's a mighty good bill—but I ain't

so damned certain as I was. It don't look
's reasonable t' me 's it did last session."

Avery left him, in the hope that a little
later on he would conclude that his present
attitude toward his daughter might under-
go like modification, with advantage to all
concerned. It was early in the evening, and
Avery concluded to step into a working-
man's club on his way to his lodgings. He
had no sooner entered the door, than someone recognized him as the candidate of a
year ago. There was an immediate demand
that he give them a speech. He had had no
thought of speaking, but the opening tempted
him, and the hand clapping was urgent.
The chairman introduced him as "the only
kid-glove member in the last Legislature
who didn't sell his soul, to monopoly, and
put a mortgage on his heavenly home at the
behest of Wall Street."

The applause which met this sally was
long sustained, and the laughter, while
hearty, was not altogether pleasant of tone.
Avery stood until there was silence. Then
he began with a quiet smile.

"Mr. Chairman and gentlemen." He

paused, and looked over the room again.
"I beg your pardon. I am accustomed to
face men only. Mr. Chairman, *ladies* and
gentlemen." There was a ripple of laughter
over the room. "Let me say how glad I am
to make that amendment, and how glad I
shall be, for one, when I am able to make it
in the body to which I have the honor to
belong—the Legislature." Some one said:
"ah, there," but he did not pause. "You
labor men have taken the right view of it in
this club. There is not a question, not one,
in all the domain of labor or legislation which
does not strike at woman's welfare as vitally
as it does at man's; not one." There was
feeble applause. "But I will go further. I
will say, there is not only not an economic
question which is not *as* vital to her, but it
is far *more* vital than it is to man. The very
fact of her present legal status rests upon
the other awful fact of her absolute financial
dependence upon men." Someone laughed,
and Avery fired up. "This one fact has
made sex maniacs of men, and peopled this
world with criminals, lunatics, and liars!
This one fact! This one fact!"

His intensity had at last forced silence, and quieted those members who were at first inclined to take as a gallant joke his opening remarks. "Let me take a text, for what I want to say to you on the economic question, from the Bible.

"Oh, give us a rest!"

"Suffer little children!"

"Remember the Sabbath day!" and like derisive calls, mingled with a laugh and distinct hisses. The gavel beat in vain; Avery waited. At last there was silence, and he said: "I was not joking. The fact that you all know me as a free-thinker misled you; but although I did say that I wished to take as a sort of text a passage from the Bible, I was in earnest. This is the text: 'The rich man's wealth is his strong city; the destruction of the poor is their poverty.' Again there was a laugh, with a different ring to it, and clapping of hands.

"I think that I may assume," he went on, "that no audience before which I am likely to appear, will suspect me of accepting the Bible as altogether admirable. Some of the prophets and holy men of old, as I read of their doings in the scriptures, always impress me as having been long overdue at the penitentiary."

There was laughter and applause at this sally, and the intangible something which emanates from an audience which tells a speaker that he now has a mental grasp upon his hearers, made itself felt. The slight air of resentment which arose when he had said that he should refer for his authority to the Bible subsided, and he went on.

"But notwithstanding these facts and opinions, one sometimes finds in the Bible things that are true. Sometimes they are not only true, but they are also good. Again they are good in fact, in sentiment, and in diction. Now when this sort of conjunction occurs, I am strongly moved to drop for the time such differences as I may have with other portions and sentiments, and give due credit where credit is due.

Therefore, when I find in the tenth chapter of Proverbs this: "The rich man's wealth is his strong city; the destruction of the poor, is their poverty," I shake hands with the

author, and travel with him for this trip at
least. The prophet does not say that their
destruction is ignorance, or vice, or sin, or
any of the ordinary blossoms of poverty
which it is the fashion to refer to as its root.
He tells us the truth — the destruction of
the poor *is* their *poverty*.

And who are the poor? Are they not
those who, in spite of their labor, their worth,
and their value to the state as good citizens
are still dependent upon the good-will — the
charity, I had almost said — of someone else
who has power over the very food they have
earned a hundred times over, and the miserable rags they are allowed to wear instead of
the broadcloth they have earned? Are they
not those who, because of economic conditions, are suppliants where they should be
sovereign citizens, dependents where they
should be free and independent and self-
respecting persons?"

"Right you are!"

"Drive it home!" came with the applause
from the audience.

"Are they not those who must obey op-
pressive laws made by those who legislate

against the helpless and in favor of the powerful? Are they not those whose voices are silenced by subjection, whose wishes and needs are trampled beneath the feet of the controlling class?"

The applause was ready now and instant. Avery paused. There was silence. "And who are these?" he asked, and paused again.

"What class of people more than any other — more than all others — fits and fills each and every one of these queries?"

"Laboring men!" shouted several. "All of us!"

"No," said Avery, "you are wrong. To all of you — to all so-called laboring men they do apply; but more than to these, in more insidious ways, do they apply to laboring women. To all women, in fact; for no matter how poor a man is, his wife and daughters are poorer; no matter how much of a dependent he is, the woman is more so, for she is the dependent of a dependent, the serf of a slave, the chattel of a chattel! The suppliant, not only for work and wage, but the suppliant at the hands of sex power for equality with even the man who is under the feet and the tyranny of wealth. They share together that tyranny and poverty, but he thrusts upon her alone the added outrage of sex subjugation and legal disability." He paused, and held up his hand. Then he said, slowly, making each word stand alone: —

"And I tell you, gentlemen, with my one term's experience in the Legislature and what it has taught me — I tell you that there is no outrage which wealth and power can commit upon man that it cannot and does not commit doubly upon woman! There is no cruelty upon all this cruel earth half so terrible as the tyranny of sex! And again, I tell you that to woman every man is a capitalist in wealth and in power, and I reiterate: — the destruction of the poor is their *poverty*. It has been doubly woman's destruction. Her absolute financial dependence upon men has given him the power and — alas, that I should be compelled to say it! — the will, to deny her all that is best and loftiest in life, and even to crush out of her the love of liberty and the dignity of char-

acter which cares for the better things.
Look at her education! Look at the disgraceful 'annexes' and side shifts which are
made to prevent our sisters from acquiring
even the same, or as good, an education as we
claim for ourselves. Look —" He paused
and lowered his voice. "Look at the awful,
the horrible, the beastly laws we pass for
women, while we carefully keep them in a
position where they cannot legislate for themselves. Do you know there is no law in any
state—and no legislature would dare try to
pass one — which would bind a ten-year-old
boy to any contract which he might have been
led, driven, or coaxed into, or have volun-
tarily made, if that contract should henceforth deprive him of all that gives to him
the comforts, joys, or decencies of life! All
men hold that such a boy is not old enough
to make such a contract. That any one
older than he, who leads him into a crime
or misdemeanor, or the transfer of property,
or his personal rights and liberty, is guilty of
legal offence. The boy is without blame,
and his contract is absolutely void — illegal.

But in more than one state we hold that

a little girl of ten may make the most fatal
contract ever made by or for woman, and
that she is old enough to be held legally
responsible for her act and for her judgment. The one who leads her into it,
though he be forty, fifty, or sixty years old,
is guiltless before the law. I tell you,
gentlemen, there is no crime possible to hu-
manity that is as black as that infamous law,
sought to be re-enacted by our own state at
this very time, and which has already passed
one house!" He explained, as delicately as
he could, the full scope and meaning of the
bill. Surprise, consternation, swept over the
room. Men, a few of whom had heard of
the bill before, but had given it scant attention, saw a horror and disgust in the eyes of
the women which aroused for the first time
in their minds, a flickering sense of the
enormity of such a measure. No one present was willing that any woman should believe him guilty of approving such legislation, and yet Avery impressed anew upon
them that the bill had passed one house
with a good majority. On his way out of
the room, a tall girl stepped to his side.

For the moment he had not recognized her. It was Francis King. She looked straight at him.

"Did my father vote for that bill?" she asked, without a prelude of greeting. Avery hesitated.

"Oh, is it you, Miss King?" he asked, "I did not see you before. Do you come here often?"

"Not very," she said, still looking at him, and with fire gathering in her eyes. "Did my father vote for that bill?" she repeated.

"Ah — I — to tell you the truth," began Avery, but she put out her hand and caught firm hold of his arm.

"Did my father vote for that bill?" she insisted, and Avery said: —

"Yes, I'm sorry to say, he did, Miss King; but — so many did, you know. The fact is—"

Her fingers grasped his arm like a vice, and her lips were drawn. "Did Ettie's pa?" she demanded.

Avery saw the drift of her thought.

"God forgive him! yes," he said, and his own eyes grew troubled and sympathetic.

"God may forgive him if he's a mind to,"
exclaimed Francis, "but I don't want no
such God around me, if he does. Any God
that wants to forgive men for such work as
that ain't fit to associate with no other kind
of folks *but* such men; but I don't mean to
allow a good little girl like Ettie to live in
the same house with a beast if I know it.
She shan't go home again now, not if her pa
begs on his knees. He ain't fit to wipe her
shoes. 'N my pa!" she exclaimed, scornfully. "My pa talkin' about Ettie being
bad, and settin' bad examples for decent
girls! Him a talkin'! Him livin' in the same
house with my little sister 'n me! Him!"
The girl was wrought to a frenzy of scorn,
and contempt, and anger. They had passed
out with the rest into the street.

"Shall I walk home with you?" asked
Avery. "Are you alone?"

"Yes, I'm alone," she said, with a little
dry sob. "I'm alone, an' I ain't goin' home
any more. Not while he lives there. It's
no decent place for a girl — living in the
house with a man like that. I ain't goin'
home. I'm goin' to—" It rushed over her

brain that she had no other place to go. She held her purse in her hand; it had only two dollars and a few cents in it. She had bought her new dress with the rest. Her step faltered, but her eyes were as fiery and as hard as ever.

"You'd better go home," said Avery, softly. "It will only be the harder for you, if you don't. I'm sorry—"

She turned on him like a tigress. They were in Union Square now. "Even *you* think it is all right for good girls to be under the control and live with men like that! Even *you* think I ought to go home, an' let him boss me an' make rules fer me, an' me pretend to like it an believe as he does, an' look up to him, an' think his way's right an' best! Even *you!*"

"No, no," said Avery, softly. "You must be fair, Miss King. I don't think it's right; but—but—I said it was best just now, for— what else can you do?" The girl was facing him as they stood near the fountain in the middle of the square.

"That's just what I was meaning to show to-night when I said what I did to the club,

of the financial dependence of women; it
is their destruction; it destroys their self-
respect; it forces them to accept a moral
companionship which they'd scorn if they
dared; it forces them to seem to condone
and uphold such things themselves; it
forces them to be the companions and subor-
dinates of degraded moral natures, that hold
wives and daughters to a code which they
will not apply to themselves, and which they
seek to make void for other wives and
daughters; it —"

"You told me to go home," she said, stubbornly. "I'm not goin'! I make money
enough to live on. I always spent it on — on
things to wear; but — but I can live on it, an'
I'm goin' to. I ain't goin' to live in the
house with no such a man. He ain't *fit* to
live with. I won't tell ma an' the girls —
yet; not till — "

She paused, and peered toward the clock
in the face of the great stone building across
the street. "Do you think it's too late fer
me t' talk a minute with Miss Gertrude?"
she asked, with her direct gaze, again.

"She'd let me stay there one night, I

guess, n' she'd tell me — I c'd talk to her some."

"If you won't go home," he said, slowly, "I suppose it would be best for you to go there, but — it is rather late. Go home for to-night, Miss Francis! I wish you would. Think it over to-night, please. Let me take you home to-night. Go to Miss Gertrude to-morrow, and talk it over." His tone had grown gentle and more tender than he knew. He took the hand she had placed on his arm in his own, and tried to turn toward her street. She held stubbornly back. "For my sake, to please me — because I think it is best — won't you go home to-night?" She looked at him again, and a haze came in her eyes. She did not trust herself to speak, but she turned toward her own street, and they walked silently down the square. His hand still held her own as it lay on his arm.

"Thank you," he said, and pressed her fingers more firmly for an instant and then released them. He had taken his glove off in the hall and had not replaced it. When they reached the door of her father's house, she suddenly grasped his ungloved hand and kissed it, and ran sobbing up the steps and into the house without a word.

"Poor girl," thought Avery, "she is not herself to-night. She has never respected nor loved her father much, but this was a phase of his nature she had not suspected before. Poor child! I hope Gertrude—" and in the selfishness of the love he bore for Gertrude, he allowed his thoughts to wander, and it did not enter his mind to place anything deeper than a mere emotional significance upon the conduct of the intense, tall, dark-eyed girl who had just left him.

He did not dream that at that moment she lay face down on her bed sobbing as if her heart would break, and yet, that a strange little flutter of happiness touched her heart as she held her gloved hand against her flushed cheek or kissed it in the darkness. It was the hand Avery had held so long within his own, as it lay upon his arm. At last the girl drew the glove off, and going to her drawer, took out her finest handkerchief and lay the glove within, wrapping it softly and carefully. She was breathing

hard, and her face was set and pained.
At two o'clock she had fallen asleep, and
under her tear-stained cheek there was a
glove folded in a bit of soft cambric.
Poor Francis King! The world is a sorry
place for such as you, and even those who
would be your best friends often deal the
deadliest wounds. Poor Francis King!
Has life nothing to offer you but a worn
glove and a tear-stained bit of cambric?
Is it true? Need it be true? Is there no
better way? Have we built your house
with but one door, and with no window?
Smile at the fancies of your sleep, child;
to-morrow will bring memory, reality,
and tears. You are a woman now. Yes-
terday you were but an unformed, strong-
willed girl. Poor Francis King! sleep late
to-morrow, and dream happily if you can.
Poor Francis King, to-morrow is very near!

XI.

"Gertrude!" called out her mother to the girl, as she passed the library door. "Gertrude! come in, your father and I wish to talk with you."

"Committee meeting?" laughed Gertrude, as she took a seat beside her father. It had grown to be rather a joke in the family to speak of Mr. Avery's calls as committee meetings, and Mr. Foster had tried vainly to tease his daughter about it.

"In my time," he would say, "we did not go a courting to get advice. We went for kisses. I never discussed any more profound topic with my sweetheart than love —and perhaps poetry and music. Sometimes, as I sit and listen to you two, I can't half believe that you are lovers. It's so perfectly absurd. You talk about everything on earth. It's a deal more like—why I should have looked upon that sort of thing

as a species of committee meeting, in my
day."

Gertrude had laughed and said something
about thinking that love ought to enter into
and run through all the interests of life, and
not be held merely as a thing apart. All
women had a life to live. All would not
have the love. So the first problem was one
of life and its work. The love was only a
phase of this. But her father had gone on
laughing at her about her queer love-making.

"Committee meeting?" asked she, again,
as she glanced at her father, smiling dryly.
Her mother answered first.

"Yes—no—partly. Your father wanted
to speak to you about—he thinks you should
not be seen with, or have those girls—You
tell her yourself, dear," she said, appealing
to her husband. Mr. Foster was fidgeting
about in his chair; he had not felt comfortable before. He was less so now, for Gertrude had turned her face full upon him, and
her hand was on his sleeve.

"Well, there's nothing to tell, Gertrude,"
he said. "I guess you can understand it
without a scene. I simply don't want to

see those girls—that King girl and her
friend—about here any more. It won't do.
It simply won't do at all. You'll be talked
about. Of course, I know it is all very kind
of you, and all that, and that you don't mean
any harm; but men always have drawn, and
they always will draw, unpleasant conclu-
sions. They may sympathize with that sort
of girls, but they simply won't stand having
their own women folks associate with them.
The test of the respectability of a woman,
is whether a man of position will marry her
or not. A man's respectable if he's out of
jail. A woman if she is marriageable or
married. Now, unfortunately, that little
Berton girl is neither the one nor the other,
and its going to make talk if you are seen
with her again. She must stay away from
here, too."

There had come a most unusual tone of
protest into his voice as he went on, but he
had looked steadily at a carved paper knife,
which he held in his hand, and with which
he cut imaginary leaves upon the table.
There was a painful silence. Gertrude
thought she did not remember having ever

before heard her father speak so sharply.
She glanced at her mother, but Katherine
Foster had evidently made up her mind to
leave this matter entirely in the hands of
her husband.

"Do you mean, papa, that you wish me to
tell that child, Ettie Berton, not to come
here any more, and that I must not befriend
her?" asked Gertrude, in an unsteady voice.

"Befriend her all you've a mind to,"
responded her father, heartily. "Certainly.
Of course. But don't have her come here,
and don't you be seen with her, nor the other
one again. You can send James or Susan
—better not send Susan though—send
James with money or anything you want to
give her. Your mother tells me you are
paying the Berton girl's board. That's all
right if you want to, but—your mother has
told me the whole outrageous story, and that
cashier ought to be shot, but—"

"But instead of helping make the public
opinion which would make him less, and
Ettie more, respectable, you ask me to help
along the present infamous order of things!
Oh, papa! don't ask that of me! I have

never willingly done anything in my life that
I knew you disapproved. Don't ask me to
help crush that child now, for I cannot. I
cannot desert her now. Don't ask that of
me, papa. Why do men—even you good
men—make it so hard, so almost impossible
for women to be kind to each other? What
has Ettie done that such as we should hold
her to account. She is a mere child. Fourteen years old in fact, but not over ten in
feeling or judgment. She has been deceived
by one who fully understood. She did not.
And yet *even you* ask me to hold her responsible! Oh, papa, don't!" She slipped onto
her father's knee and took his face in her
hands and kissed his forehead. She had
never in her life stood against her father or
seemed to criticise him before. It hurt her
and it vexed him. A little frown came on
his face.

"Katherine," he said, turning to his wife,
"I wish you'd make Gertrude understand
this thing rationally. *You* always have."
Mrs. Foster glanced at her daughter and
then at her husband. She smiled.

"I always have, what dear?" she asked.

"Understood these things as I do—as everyone does," said her husband. "You never took these freaks that Gertrude is growing into, and—"

The daughter winced and sat far back on her father's knee. Her mother did not miss the action. She smiled at the girl, but her voice was steady, and less light than usual.

"No, I never took freaks, as you say, but what I thought of things, or how I may or may not have understood them, dear, no one ever inquired, no one ever cared to know. That I acted like other people, and acquiesced in established opinions, went without saying. That was expected of me. That I did. Gertrude belongs to another generation, dear. She cannot be so colorless as we women of my time—"

Her husband laughed.

" Colorless, is good, by Jove! *You* colorless indeed!" He looked admiringly at his wife. " Why, Katherine, you have more color and more sense now than any half dozen girls of this generation. Colorless indeed!"

Mrs. Foster smiled. " Don't you think my cheerful, easy reflection of your own shades

of thought or mind have always passed cur-
rent as my own? Sometimes I fancy that is
true, and that — it is easier and — pleasanter
all around. But — " she paused. "It was
not my color, my thought, my opinions, myself. It was an echo, dear; a pleasant echo
of yourself which has so charmed you. It
was not I."

Gertrude felt uneasy, and as if she were
lifting a curtain which had been long drawn.
Her father turned his face towards her and
then toward her mother.

"In God's name what does all this mean?"
he asked. "Are you, the most level-headed
woman in the world, intending to uphold
Gertrude in this — suicidal policy — her —
this — absurd nonsense about that girl?"

Gertrude's eyes widened. She slowly
arose from his knee. The revelation as to
her father's mental outlook was, to her more
sensitive and developed nature, much what
the one had been to Francis King that night
at the club.

"Oh, papa," she said softly. "I am so
sorry for — so sorry — for us all. We seem
so far apart, and — "

"John Martin agrees with me perfectly," said her father, hotly. "I talked with him to-day. He —"

Gertrude glanced at her mother, and there was a definite curl upon her lip. "Mr. Martin," she said slowly, "is not a conscience for me. He and I are leagues apart, papa. We —"

"More's the pity," said her father, as he arose from his chair. He moved toward the door.

"I've said my say, Gertrude. It's perfectly incomprehensible to me what you two are aiming at. But what I know is this: you must *do* my way in this particular case, think whatever you please. You know very well I would not ask it except for your own good. I don't like to interfere with your plans, but — you must give that girl up." He spoke kindly, but Gertrude and her mother sat silent long after he had gone. The twilight had passed into darkness. Presently Katherine's voice broke the silence:—

"Shall you float with the tide, daughter, or shall you try to swim up stream?" She

was thinking of the first talk they had ever
had on these subjects, nearly two years ago
now, but the girl recognized the old question. She stood up slowly and then with
quick steps came to her mother's side.

"Don't try to swim with me, mamma. It
only makes it harder for me to see you hurt
in the struggle. Don't try to help me any
more when the eddies come. Float, mamma;
I shall swim. I shall! I shall! And while
my head is above the waves that poor little
girl shall not sink."

She was stroking Katherine's hair, and her
mother's hand drew her own down to a soft
cheek.

"Am I right, mother?" she asked, softly.
"If you say I am right, it is enough. My
heart will ache to seem to papa to do
wrong, but I can bear it better than I could
bear my own self-contempt. Am I right,
mamma?"

Her mother drew her hand to her lips,
and then with a quick action she threw both
arms about the girl and whispered in her
ear: "I shall go back to the old way. Swim
if you can, daughter. You are right. If

only you are strong enough. That is the
question. If only you are strong enough.
I am not. I shall remain in the old way."

There was a steadiness and calm in her
voice which matched oddly enough with the
fire in her eyes and the flush on her cheeks.

"Little mother, little mother," murmured
Gertrude, softly, as she stroked her mother's
hand. Then she kissed her and left the
room. "With her splendid spirit, that *she*
should be broken on the wheel!" the girl
said aloud to herself, when she had reached
her own room. She did not light the gas,
but sat by the window watching the passers-
by in the street.

"Why should papa have sent me to college," she was thinking, "where I matched
my brains and thoughts with men, if I was
to stifle them later on, and subordinate them
to brains I found no better than my own?
Why should my conscience be developed, if
it must not be used; if I must use as my
guide the conscience of another? Why
should I have a separate and distinct nature
in all things, if I may use only that part of
it which conforms to those who have not

the same in type or kind? I will do what
seems right to myself. I shall not desert —"

She laid her cheek in her hand and sighed.
A new train of thought was rising. It had
never come to her before.

"It is my father's money. He says I may
send it, but I may not — it is my father's
money. He has the right to say how it
may be used, and — and —" (the blood
was coming into her face) "I have nothing
but what he gives me. He wants a pleasant
home; he pays for it. Susan and James,
and the rest, he hires to conduct the labor
of the house. If they do not do it to please
him — if they are not willing to — they
have no right to stay, and then to complain.
For his social life at home he has mamma
and me. If he wants —" She was walking
up and down the room now. "Have we a
right to dictate? We have our places in
his home. We are not paid wages like
James and Susan, but — but — we are given
what we have; we are dependent. He has
never refused us anything — any sum we
wanted — but he can. It is in his power,
and really we do not know but that he

should. Perhaps we spend too much. We
do not know. What can he afford? I do
not know. What can *I* afford?" She
spread her hands out before her, palms up,
in the darkness. She could see them by the
flicker of the electric light in the street.

"They are empty," she said, aloud, "and
they are untrained, and they are helpless.
They are a pauper's hands." She smiled a
little at the conceit, and then, slowly: "It
sounds absurd, almost funny, but it is true.
A pauper in lace and gold! I am over
twenty-two. I am as much a dependent
and a pauper as if I were in a poorhouse.
Love and kindness save me! They have
not saved Ettie, nor Francis. When the
day came they were compelled to yield utterly, or go. They can work, and I? I
am a dependent. Have I a right to stand
against the will and pleasure of my father,
when by doing so I compel him to seem to
sustain and support that which he disap-
proves? Have I a right to do that?"

She was standing close to the window
now, and she put her hot face against the
glass. "The problem is easy enough, if all

think alike — if one does not think at all;
but now? I cannot follow my own conscience and my father's too. We do not
think alike. Is it right that I should, to
buy his approval and smiles, violate my
own mind, and brain, and heart? But is it
right for me to violate *his* sense of what is
right, while I live upon the lavish and loving
bounty which he provides?" And so, with
her developed conscience, and reason, and
individuality, Gertrude had come to face
the same problem, which, in its more brutal
form, had resulted so sorrowfully for the two
girls whom she had hoped to befriend. The
ultimate question of individual domination
of one by another, with the purse as the
final appeal — and even this strong and fortunate girl wavered. "Shall I swim, after
all? Have I the right to try?" she asked
herself.

XII.

When Francis King told Mr. Avery that she could and would leave her father's home and live upon the money she earned, and had heretofore looked upon as merely a resource to save her pride, she did not take into consideration certain very important facts, not the least of which was, perhaps, that her presence at the store was not wholly a pleasant thing for the cashier to contemplate under existing circumstances.

Francis King was not a diplomat. The cashier was not a martyr. These two facts, added to the girl's scornful eyes, rendered the position in the trimming department far less secure than she had grown to believe.

So when she came to the little room which Gertrude Foster had provided as a temporary home for Ettie Berton, she felt that

she came as a help and protector and not at
all as a possible encumbrance.

"I've had a terrible blow-out with pa,"
she said, bitterly. "I can't go home any
more if I wanted to — and I don't want to.
I told him what I thought of him, and of
your — and of the kind of men that make
mean laws they are ashamed to have their
own folks know about and live by. He was
awful mad. He said laws was none o' my
business, and he guessed men knew best
what was right an' good for women."

"Of course they do," said Ettie with her
ever ready acquiescence. "I reckon you
didn't want t' deny *that*, did you Fan? You
'n your pa must a' shook hands for once
anyhow," she laughed. "How'd it feel?
Didn't you like agreein' with him once?"

Francis looked at the child — this pitiful
illustration of the theory of yielding acquiescence; this legitimate blossom of the tree
of ignorance and soft-hearted dependence;
this poor little dwarf of individuality; this
helpless echo of masculine measures, meth-
ods, and morals — and wondered vaguely why
it was that the more helpless the victim,

the more complete her disaster, the more
certain was she to accept, believe in, and
support the very cause and root of her un-
doing.

Francis King's own mental processes were
too disjointed and ill-formulated to enable
her to express the half-formed thoughts
that came to her. Her heart ached for her
little friend to whom to-day was always
welcome, and to whom to-morrow never appeared a possibility other than that it would
be sunshiny, and warm, and comfortable.

Francis saw a certain to-morrow which
should come to Ettie, far more clearly than
did the child herself, and seeing, sighed.
Her impulse was to argue the case hotly
with Ettie, as she had done with her father;
but she looked at her face again, and then,
as a sort of safety-valve for her own emo-
tion, succinctly said: "Ettie Berton, you
are the biggest fool I ever saw."

Ettie clapped her hands.

" Right you are, says Moses!" she exclaimed, laughing gleefully, "and you like
me for it. Folks with sense like fools.
Sense makes people so awful uncomfortable.

Say, where'd you get that bird on your hat?
Out 'o stock? Did that old mean thing
make you pay full price? Goodness! how
I do wish I could go back t' store!"

"Ettie, how'd you like for me to come
here an' live with you? Do you 'spose Miss
Gertrude would care?"

"Hurrah for Cleveland!" exclaimed Ettie,
springing to her feet and throwing her arms
about Francis. "Hurrah for Grant! Gracious, but I'm glad! I'm just so lonesome
I had to make my teeth ache for company,"
she rattled on. "Miss Gertrude 'll be glad,
too. She said she wisht I had somebody 't
take care of me. But, gracious! I don't need
that. They ain't nothing to do but just set
still n' wait. It's the waitin' now that makes
me so lonesome. I want t' hurry 'n get
back t' the store, 'n —"

She noticed Francis's look of surprise, not
unmixed with frank scorn; but she did not
rightly interpret it.

"My place ain't gone is it, Fan?" she
asked, in real alarm. "He said he'd keep it
for me."

"Ettie Berton, you are the biggest fool I

ever saw," said Francis, again, this time with
a touch of hopelessness and pathos in her
voice, and at that moment there was a rap
at the door. It was one of the cash girls
from the store. She handed Francis a note,
and while Ettie and the visitor talked gaily
of the store, Francis read and covered her
pale face with her trembling hands. She
was discharged "owing to certain necessary
changes to be made in the trimming department." She went and stood by the window
with her back to the two girls. She understood the matter perfectly, and she did not
dare trust herself to speak. It could not be
helped, she thought, and why let Ettie know
that she had brought this disaster upon her
friend, also. Francis was trying to think.
She was raging within herself. Then it
came to her that she had boldly asserted
that she would help protect and support
Ettie. Now she was penniless, helpless,
and homeless herself. There were but two
faces that stood out before her as the faces
of those to whom she could go for help and
counsel, and she was afraid to go to even

these. She was ashamed, humiliated, uncertain.

She supposed that Gertrude Foster could help her if she would. She had that vague miscomprehension of facts which makes the less fortunate look upon the daughters of wealth and luxury and love as possessed of a magic wand which they need but stretch forth to compass any end. She did not dream that at that very moment Gertrude Foster was revolving exactly the same problem in her own mind, and reaching out vainly for a solution. "What shall I do? what ought I to do? what can I do?" were questions as real and immediate to Gertrude, in the new phase of life and thought which had come to her, as they were to Francis in her extremity. It is true that the greater part of the problem in Francis's mind dealt with the physical needs of herself and her little friend, and with her own proud and fierce anger toward her father and the cashier. It is also true that these features touched Gertrude but lightly; but the highest ideals, beliefs, aspirations, and love of her soul were in conflict within

her, and the basis of the conflict was the
same with both girls. Each had, in following the best that was within herself, come
into violent contact with established prejudice and prerogative, and each was beating
her wings, the one against the bars of
a gilded cage draped lovingly in silken
threads, and the other was feeling her help-
lessness where iron and wrath unite to hold
their prey.

The other face that arose before Francis
brought the blood back to her face. She
had not seen him since she had kissed his
hand that night, and she wondered what he
thought of her. She felt ashamed to go to
him for help. She had talked so confidently
to him that night of her own powers, and of
her determination that Ettie should not
again live under the same roof, and be subject to the will of the father whom she insisted was a disgrace to the child.

"I reckon *he* could get me another place
to work—in a store," she thought. "But—"
She shook her head, and a fierce light came
into her eyes. She had learned enough to
know that a girl who had left home under

the wrath of her father, would best not
appeal for a situation under the protection
and recommendation of a young gentleman
not of her own caste or condition in life.
She thought of all this and of what it implied, and it seemed to her that her heart
would burst with shame and rage.

Was she not a human being? Were there
not more reasons than one why another
human unit should be kind to her and help
her? If she were a boy all this shame would
be lifted from her shoulders, all these sus-
picions and repression and artificial barriers
would be gone. She wondered if she could
not get a suit of men's clothes, and so solve
the whole trouble. No one would then
question her own right of individual and
independent action or thought. No one
would then think it commendable for her to
be a useless atom, subordinating her whole
individuality to one man, to whose mental
and moral tone she must bend her own,
until such time as he should turn her over
to some other human entity, whereupon she
would be required to readjust all her mental
and moral belongings to accommodate the

new master. How comfortable it would be,
she thought, to go right on year after year,
growing into and out of herself. Expanding
her own nature, and finding the woman of
to-morrow the outcome of the girl of yester-
day. She had once heard a teacher explain
about the chameleon with its capacity to
adjust itself to and take on the color of
other objects. It floated into her mind that
girls were expected to be like chameleons.
Instead of being John King's daughter,
with, of course, John King's ideas, status
and aspirations, or William Jones's wife —
now metamorphosed into a tepid reflex of
William Jones himself — she thought how
pleasant it would be to continue to be Francis King, and not feel afraid to say so. The
idea fascinated her. Yes, she would get a
suit of men's clothes, and henceforth have
and feel the dignity of individual responsi-
bility and development. She slipped out of
the room and into the street. She thought
she would order the clothes as if "for a
brother just my size." She could pay for a
cheap suit. She paused in front of a shop
window, and the sight of her own face in a

glass startled her. She groaned aloud. She
knew as she looked that she was too handsome to pass for a man. It was a woman's
face. Then, too, how could she live with
and care for Ettie?

"No, *I'll* have to go to *them* for help,"
she said, desperately to herself, and turning,
faced Selden Avery coming across the
street. The color flew into her face, but
she saw at a glance that he did not think of
their last meeting — or, at least, not of its
ending. "I was just wishing I could see
you and Miss Gertrude," she said, bluntly,
her courage coming back when he paused,
recognizing that she wished to speak further
with him than a mere greeting.

"Were you?" he said, smiling. "Our
thoughts were half-way the same then, for I
was wishing to see her, too."

She thought how pleasant and soft his
voice was, and she tried to modify the tones
of her own.

"I was goin' t' ask you — her — what to
do about — about something," she said, fal-
teringly.

"So was I," he smiled back, showing his

perfect teeth. "She will have to be very,
very wise to advise us both, will she not?
Shall we go to her now? And together?
Perhaps our united wisdom may solve both
your problem and mine. Three people
ought to be three times as wise as one,
oughtn't they?"

XIII.

When Gertrude came forward to meet
Selden Avery and Francis King, she felt
the disapproving eyes of her father fixed
upon her. It was a new and a painful
sensation. It made her greeting less free
and frank than usual, and both Avery and
Francis felt without being able to analyze it.

"She don't like me to be with him,"
thought Francis, and felt humiliated and
hurt.

"Surely Gertrude cannot doubt *me*," was
Avery's mental comment, and a sore spot in
his heart, left by a comment made at the
club touching Gertrude's friendship for this
same tall, fiery girl at his side, made itself
felt again. John Martin exchanged glances
with Gertrude's father. Avery saw, and
seeing, resented what he believed to be its
meaning.

The three men bowed rather stiffly to each

other. Francis felt that she was, somehow,
to blame. She wished that she had not come.
She longed to go, but did not know what to
say nor how to start. The situation was
awkward for all. Gertrude wished for and
yet dreaded the entrance of her mother.

Avery felt ashamed to explain, but he began as if speaking to Gertrude and ended
with a look of challenge at the two men
facing him. "I chanced to meet Miss King
in the street and as both of us stood in need
of advice from you," he was trying to smile
unconcernedly, "we came up the avenue
together."

There was a distinct look of displeasure
and disapproval upon Mr. Foster's face,
while John Martin took scant pains to
conceal his disgust. He, also, had heard,
and repeated, the club gossip to Gertrude's
father.

"If good advice is what you want particularly," said Mr. Foster, slowly, "I don't
know but that I might accommodate you.
I hardly think Gertrude is in a position to —
to —"

The bell rang sharply and in an instant

the little cash girl from the store rushed in gasping for breath. ·

"Come quick! quick! Ettie is killed! She fell down stairs and then — oh, something *awful* happened! I don't know what it was. The doctor is there. He sent me here, 'cause Ettie cried and called for you!"

She was looking at Gertrude, who started toward the door.

"Go back and tell the doctor that Miss Foster cannot come," said her father, rising.

"Certainly not, I should hope," remarked John Martin under his breath; "the most preposterous idea!" Gertrude paused. She was looking at her father with appeal in her face. Then her eyes fell upon the tense lips and piercing gaze of Francis King who, half way to the street door, had turned and was looking first from one to the other.

"Papa," said Gertrude, "don't say that. I must go. It is right that I should, and I must." Then with outstretched hands, "I want to go, papa! I need to. Don't — "

"You will do nothing of the kind, Gertrude. It is outrageous. What business have you got with that kind of girls? I *asked* you to stop having them come here, and I told you to let them alone. I am perfectly disgusted with Avery, here, for — " He had thought Francis was gone. The drapery where she had turned to hear what Gertrude would say hid her from him. " *With that kind of girls!*" was ringing in her ears.

"I hope when you are married *that* is not the sort of society he is going to surround you with. It — " Avery saw for the first time what the trouble was. He stepped quickly to Gertrude's side and slipped one arm about her. Then he took the hand she still held toward her father.

"My wife shall have her own choice. She is as capable as I to choose. I shall not interfere. She shall not find me a master, but a comrade. Gertrude is her own judge and my adviser. That is all I ask, and it is all I assume for myself as her husband — when that time comes," he added, with her hand to his lips.

Mrs. Foster entered attired for the street. The unhappy face of Francis King with wide eyes staring at Gertrude met her gaze. She

had heard what went before. "Get your
hat, Gertrude," she said. I will go with
you. It might take too long to get a carriage. Francis, come with me; Gertrude
will follow us. Come with her, my son,"
she said, to Selden Avery, and a spasm of
happiness swept over his face. She had
never called him that before. He stooped
and kissed her, and there were tears in the
young man's eyes as Mrs. Foster led Francis King away.

"I suppose it was all my fault to begin
with," said John Martin, when the door had
closed behind them. "It all started from
that visit to the Spillinis. The only way to
keep the girls of this age in —" he was going to say "in their place," but he changed
to "'where they belong,' is not to let them
find out the facts of life. Charity and religion did well enough to appease the con-
sciences of women before they had colleges,
and all that. I didn't tell you so at the time,
but I always did think it was a mistake to
send Gertrude to a college where she could
measure her wits with men. She'll never
give it up. She don't know where to stop."

Mr. Foster lighted a cigar—a thing he seldom did in the drawing-room. He handed one to John Martin.

"I guess you're right, John," he said, slowly. "She can't seem to see that graduation day ended all that. It was Katherine's idea, sending her there, though. I wanted her to go to Vassar or some girl's school like that. I don't know what to make of Katherine lately; when I come to think of it, I don't know what to make of her all along. She seems to have laid this plan from the first, college and all; but I never saw it. Sometimes I'm afraid—sometimes I almost think —" He tapped his forehead and shook his head, and John Martin nodded contemplatively, and said: "I shouldn't wonder if you are right, Fred. Too much study is a dangerous thing for women. The structure of their brains won't stand it. It is sad, very sad;" and they smoked in sympathetic silence, while James had hastened below stairs to assure Susan that he thought he'd catch himself allowing his sweetheart or wife to demean herself and disgrace him by having anything to do with a person in the position of Ettie Berton. And Susan had little doubt that James was quite right, albeit Susan felt moderately sure that in a contest of wits — after the happy day — she could be depended upon to get her own way by hook or by crook, and Susan had no vast fund of scruple to allay as to method or motive. Deception was not wholly out of Susan's line. Its necessity did not disturb her slumbers.

XIV.

Some one had sent for Ettie's father. They told him that she was dying, and he had come at once. Mr. King had gone with him. The latter gentleman did not much approve of his colleague's soft-heartedness in going. He did not know where his own daughter was, and he did not care. She had faced him in her fiery way, and angered him beyond endurance the morning after she had learned of the awful bill which he had not really originated, but which he had induced Mr. Berton to present, at the earnest behest of a social lion whose wont it was to roar mightily in the interest of virtue, but who was at the present moment engaged in lobbying vigorously in the interest of vice.

When Francis entered the sick-room with Mrs. Foster, and found the two men there, she gave one glance at the pallid, unconscious figure on the bed, and then demanded,

fiercely: "Where is the cashier? Why
didn't you bring him and — and the rest of
you who help make laws to keep him where
he is, an' — an' to put Ettie where she is?
Why didn't y' bring *all* of your kind that
helped along the job?"

Mrs. Foster had been bending over the
child on the bed. She turned.

"Don't, Francis," she said, trying to draw
the girl away. She was standing before
the two men, who were near the window.
"Don't, Francis. That can do no good. They
did not intend —"

"No'm," began Berton, awkwardly; "no'm,
I didn't once think o' *my* girl, n —" He
glanced uneasily at his colleague and then
at the face on the bed.

"Or you would never have wanted such
a law passed, I am sure," said Katherine.

"No'm, I wouldn't," he said, doggedly,
not looking at his colleague.

"Don't tell me!" exclaimed Francis.
"You don't none of you care for her. He
only cares because it is his girl an' disgraces
him. What did he do? Care for her?
No, he drove her off. That shows who

he's a-carin' for. He ain't sorry because it hurts or murders her. He never tried to make it easy for her an' say he was a lot more to blame an' — an' — a big sight worse every way than she was. He's a-howling now about bein' sorry; but he's only sorry for himself. He'd a let her starve — an' so'd *he*," she said, pointing to her father. She was trembling with rage and excitement. "I hope there is a hell! I jest hope there is! I'll be willin' to go to it myself jest t' see — "

The door opened softly and Gertrude entered, and behind her stood Selden Avery.

"That kind of girls" floated anew into Francis's brain, and the sting of the words she had heard Gertrude's father utter drove her on. "I wish to God, every man that ever lived could be torn to pieces an' — an' put under Ettie's feet. They wouldn't be fit for her to walk on — none of 'em! She never did no harm on purpose ner when she understood; an' men — men jest love to be mean!"

She felt the utter inadequacy of her words, and a great wave of feeling and a sense of baffled resentment swept over her, and she burst into tears. Gertrude tried to draw her out of the room. At the door she sobbed: "Even *her* father's jest like the rest, only — only he says it easier. He—"

"Francis, Francis," said Gertrude, almost sternly, when they were outside the sick-room. "You must not act so. It does no good, and — and you are partly wrong, besides. If—"

"I didn't mean *him*," said the girl, with her handkerchief to her eyes. "I didn't mean *him*. I know what he thinks about it. I heard him talk one night at the club. He talked square, an' I reckon he is square. But *I* wouldn't take no chances. I wouldn't marry the Angel Gabriel an' give him a chance to lord it over me!"

Gertrude smiled in spite of herself, and glanced within through the open door. There was a movement towards where the sick girl lay. "If you go in, you must be quiet," she said to Francis, and entered. Ettie had been stirring uneasily. She opened her great blue eyes, and when she saw the faces about her, began to sob aloud.

"Don't let pa scold me. I'll do his way.
I'll do — anything anybody wants. I like
to. The store —" She gave a great shriek
of agony. She had tried to move and fell
back in a convulsion. She was only partly
conscious of her suffering, but the sight was
terrible enough to sympathetic hearts, and
there was but one pair of dry eyes in the
room. The same beady, stern, hard glitter
held its place in the eyes of Mr. King.

"Serves her right," he was thinking.
"And a mighty good lesson. Bringin' disgrace on a good man's name!"

The tenacity with which Mr. King ad-
hered to the belief in, and solicitude for, a
good name, would have been touching had
it not been noticeable to the least observant
that his theory was, that the custody of that
desirable belonging was vested entirely in
the female members of a family. Nothing
short of the most austere morals could pre-
serve the family 'scutcheon if he was contemplating one side. Nothing short of a
long-continued, open, varied, and obtrusive
dishonesty and profligacy of a male member
could even dull its lustre. It was a com-

fortable code for a part of its adherents.

Had his poor, colorless, inane wife ever dared to deviate from the beaten path of social observance, Mr. King would have talked about and felt that "his honor" was tarnished. Were he to follow far less strictly the code, he would not only be sure that his own honor was intact, but if any one were to suggest to him the contrary, or that he was compromising her honor, he would have looked upon that person as lacking in what he was pleased to call "common horse-sense." He was in no manner a hypocrite. His sincerity was undoubted. He followed the beaten track. Was it not the masculine reason and logic of the ages, and was not that final? Was not all other reason and logic merely a spurious emotionalism? morbid? unwholesome? irrational?

No one would gainsay that unless it were a lunatic or a woman, which was much the same thing—and since the opinion of neither of these was valuable, why discuss or waste time with them? That was Mr. King's point of view, and he was of the opinion that he had a pretty good voting majority with him, and a voting majority was the measure of value and ethics with Representative King—when the voting majority was on his side.

When the last awful agony came to poor little Ettie Berton, and she yielded up, in pathetic terror and reluctant despair, the life which had been moulded for her with such a result almost as inevitable as the death itself, a wave of tenderness and remorse swept over her father. He buried his face in the pillow beside the poor, pretty, weak, white face that would win favor and praise by its cheerful ready acquiescence no more, and wept aloud. This impressed Representative King as reasonable enough, under all the circumstances, but when Ettie's father intimated later to Francis that he had been to blame, and that, perhaps, after all, Ettie *was* only the legitimate result of her training and the social and legal conditions which he had helped to make and sustain, Representative King curled his lip scornfully and remarked that in his opinion Tom Berton never could be relied on to be anything but a damned fool in the long run. He was a splendid "starter." Always opened up well in any line; but unless someone else held the reins after that the devil would be to pay and no mistake.

Francis heard; and, hearing, shut tight her lips and with her tear-swollen eyes upon the face of her dead friend, swore anew that to be disgraced by the presence of a father like that was more than she could bear. She could work or she could die; but there was nothing on this earth, she felt, that would be so impossible, so disgraceful, as for her to ever again acknowledge his authority as her guide.

"Come home with me to-night, Francis," said Mrs. Foster. "We will think of a plan —"

"I'm goin' to stay right here," said the girl, with a sob and a shiver; for she had all the horror and fear of the dead that is common to her type and her inexperience. "I'm goin' to stay right here. I can't go home, an' I'm discharged at the store. Ettie told me her rent was paid for this month. I'll take her place here an'— an' try to find another place to work."

Mrs. Foster realized that to stay in that room would fill the girl with terror, but she felt, too, that she understood why Francis would not go home with her. "That kind of girls" from Mr. Foster's lips had stung this fierce, sensitive creature to the quick. A week ago she would have been glad indeed to accept Katherine Foster's offer. Now she would prefer even this chamber of death, where the odors made her ill, and the thoughts and imaginings would insure to her sleepless nights of unreasoning fear. Her father did not ask her to go home. Representative King believed in representing. Was not his family a unit? And was he not the figure which stood for it? It had never been his custom to ask the members of his household to do things. He told them that he wanted certain lines of action followed. That was enough. The thought and the will of that ideal unit, "the family," vested in the person of Mr. King and he proposed to represent it in all things.

If by any perverse and unaccountable mental process there was developed a personality other than and different from

his own, Representative King did not pro-
pose to be disturbed in his home-life — as he
persisted in calling the portion of his existence where he was able to hold the iron
hand of power ever upon the throat of
submission — to the extent of having such
unseemly personality near him.

In her present mood he did not want
Francis at home. Representative King was
a staunch advocate of harmony and unity in
the family life. He was of opinion that
where timidity and dependence say "yes" to
all that power suggests, that there dwelt
unity and harmony. That is to say, he
held to this idea where it touched the sexes
and their relation to each other in what he
designated an ideal domestic life. In all
other relations he held far otherwise—unless
he chanced to be on the side of power
and had a fair voting majority. Representative King was an enthusiastic admirer of
submission—for other people. He thought
that there was nothing like self-denial to
develop the character and beauty of a nature.
It is true that his scorn was deep when he
contempleted the fact that John Berton

"had no head of his own," but then, John
Berton was a man, and a man ought to have
some self-respect. He ought to develop his
powers and come to something definite.
A definite woman was a horror. Her attrac-
tiveness depended upon her vagueness,
so Representative King thought; and if a
large voting majority was not with him in
open expression, he felt reasonably sure that
he could depend upon them in secret session,
so to speak. Representative King was not
a linguist, but he could read between the
social and legal lines very cleverly indeed,
and finer lines of thought than these were
not for Representative King.

And so he did not ask Francis to go
home. "When she gets ready to go my
way and says so, she can come," he thought.

"When that dress gets shabby and she's
a little hungry, she'll conclude that my way
is good enough for her." He smiled at the
vision of the future "unity and harmony"
which should thus be ushered into his home
by means of a little judiciously applied dis-
cipline, and Francis took her dead friend's

place as a lodger and tried to think, between her spasms of loneliness and fears, what she should do on the morrow.

XV.

"Francis told me once at the Guild that she can make delicious bread and pastry," said Gertrude, as they drove home. "I wonder if we could not start her in a little shop of her own. She has the energy and vim to build herself a business. I doubt if she will every marry—with her experience one can hardly wonder—and there is a long life before her. Her salvation will be work; a career, success."

"A career in a pastry shop seems droll enough," smiled her mother, but—"

"I think I might influence the club to take a good deal of her stuff. We've a miserable pastry cook now," said Avery. "That would help her to get a start, and the start is always the hard part, I suppose, in a thing like that."

"That would be a splendid chance. If the members liked her things, perhaps they

would get their wives to patronize her, too,"
said Gertrude, gaily. "I'm so glad you
thought of that, but then you always think
of the right thing," she added, tenderly.
They all three laughed a little, and Avery
slipped his arm about her.

"Do I?" he asked in a voice tremulous
with happiness. "Do I, Darling? I'm so glad
you said that, for I've just been thinking
that — that I don't want to go back to
Albany without you, and — and the new
session begins in ten weeks. Darling, will
you go with me? May she, my mother?"
he asked, catching Mrs. Foster's hand in his
own. The two young people were facing
her. She sat alone on the back seat of the
closed carriage. The street lights were
beginning to blossom and flicker. The rays
fell upon the mother's face as they drove.
Her eyes were closed, and tears were on
her cheeks.

"Forgive me,. mother," said Avery,
tenderly. "Forgive me! You have gone
through so much to-day. I should have
waited; but—but I love her so. I need

her so—I need her to help me think right. Can you understand?"

Mrs. Foster moved to one side and held out both arms to her daughter.

"Sit by me," she said, huskily, and Gertrude gathered her in her young, strong arms.

"Can I understand?" half sobbed Katherine from her daughter's shoulder. "Can I understand? Oh, I do! I do! and I am so happy for you both; but she—she is *my* daughter, and it is so hard to let her go—even to you! It is so hard!"

Gertrude could not speak. She tried to look at her lover, but tears filled her eyes. She was holding her mother's hand to her lips.

"Dear little mamma," she whispered; "dear little mamma, I shall never go if it makes you unhappy—never, if it breaks my heart. But mamma, I love you more because I love him; and—"

"I know, I know," said Katherine, trying to struggle out of her heartache which held back and beyond itself a tender joy for these two. "But love is so selfish. I *am* glad. I am glad for you both—but—oh, my daughter, I love you, *I* love you!" she said, and choked down a sob to smile in the girl's eyes.

Mr. Foster was waiting for them in the library. They were late. He had been thinking.

"Well, I'm tremendously glad you're back," he said brightly, kissing his wife, and then he took Gertrude in his arms. "Sweetheart," he said, smiling down into her eyes, "if I seemed harsh to-day, I'm sorry. I only did it because I thought it was for your own good. You know that."

"Why, papa," she said, with her cheek against his own; "of course I know. Of course I understand. We all did. You don't mind if we did not see your way? You—"

"The girl is dead, dear," said Mrs. Foster, touching her husband's arm, "and—let us not talk of that now, to—to these, our children. They want your—they want to ask—they are going to be married in ten weeks?"

"The dickens!" exclaimed her father, and

held Gertrude at arm's length. "Is that so, Sweetheart?" There was a twinkle in his eyes, and he lifted her chin with one finger and then kissed her. "The dickens! Well, all I've got to say is, I'm sorry for old Martin and the rest of us," and he grasped Selden Avery's hand. "I hope you'll give up that legislative foolishness pretty soon and come back to town and live with civilized people in a civilized way. It'll be horribly lonely in New York without Gertrude, but—oh, well, its nature's way. We're all a lot of robbers. I stole this little woman away from her father, and I'm an unrepentent thief yet, am I not?" and he kissed his wife with the air of a man who feels that life is well worth living, no matter what its penalties, so long as she might be not the least of them.

"Pushed by Unseen Hands."

PRESS NOTICES OF FIRST EDITION.

BY HELEN H. GARDENER.

Boston Traveller.

Must add to her already enviable reputation. These stories have the marks of a brilliant genius; they are original in style and design, and are a new thing in literature. Realistic in the extreme, they are at the same time delightfully artistic.

New York Times.

The book is clever, dramatic, and in a literary sense has much merit.

Kansas City Times.

Helen Gardener is the most fearless motive fictionist of these times, and has given time, thought and revelation to some phases of society hitherto clothed. . . . all her writings are wholesome and profitable reading. . . .

Omaha Bee.

Highly commended from a scientific point of view by recognized scientific authority. . . . charming method of giving to her readers pleasure with profit.

The Baltimore American.

The terseness of expression, the delicacy of humor, and clever dramatic ability that have characterized some of her earlier efforts, are equally striking in this later work, which quickens the reader's thoughts toward a channel of science yearly receiving more and more attention.

Boston Globe.

So realistic as to leave no doubt of their actuality. . . . The stories are told with no apparent purpose to adorn a moral, and are the very best fiction, yet no intelligent person can finish the book without wishing to relieve the evils which surround high and low alike.

St. Louis Republic.

Bright, pointed, and full of interest. A book such as this. . . . is welcome.

Grand Rapids (Mich.) Eagle.

A book destined to meet a large audience, not only because of its author's fame, but because it has merit.

Chicago Times.

Vivid and artistic. The author is a woman of remarkable gifts and of superb courage.

New Orleans Picayune.

Fascinating to the imagination. Miss Gardener's touch is very exquisite, and she draws her mental pictures with the hand of a master, showing in a few rapid lines more sharp and attractive characteristics than many authors can in labored pages.

Inter-Ocean (Chicago).

The stories are aboundingly interesting, both from the manner of telling, and from their suggestive thoughts. The author seems always to write for some definite purpose, and that purpose to defend the right, protect the weak and helpless, and make the world wiser and better. Great wrongs could scarcely be more keenly rebuked, or great truths more forcibly stated, than by these terse stories. They are graphic in their style, elegant in their literary construction, and convey moral lessons full of health and life.

Price, Paper, 50 Cents; Cloth, $1.00.

THE COMMONWEALTH CO.,

121 FOURTH AVE., NEW YORK.

Just out—A Powerful Realistic Novel of Western Life, by Mr. Garland.

JASON EDWARDS

An Average Man,

A Story of To-day,

BY

HAMLIN GARLAND,

Author of "A Spoil of Office," "Main Traveled Roads," &c., &c.

" I swear that the builder no longer
To me shall be less than the plan,
Henceforward be guerdon and glory
And life for the average man."
— HAMLIN GARLAND.

Price, 50 Cts.

Published by

ARENA PUBLISHING CO.,

BOSTON, MASS.

FOR SALE BY THE TRADE.

www.ingramcontent.com/pod-product-compliance
Lightning Source LLC
Chambersburg PA
CBHW030547040726
47497CB00008B/2610